Snackers

Snackers

stories by

Janina Hornosty

OOLICHAN BOOKS
LANTZVILLE, BRITISH COLUMBIA, CANADA
1997

Canadian Cataloguing in Publication Data

    Hornosty, Janina, 1962-
    Snackers

ISBN 0-88982-163-1
I. Title.
PS8565.O6699S6 1997C813'.54   C97-910280-4
PR9199.3.H5952S6 1997

We acknowledge the support of the Canada Council for the Arts for our publishing programme.

THE CANADA COUNCIL | LE CONSEIL DES ARTS
FOR THE ARTS | DU CANADA
SINCE 1957 | DEPUIS 1957

Grateful acknowledgement is also made to the BC Ministry of Tourism, Small Businesss and Culture for their financial support.

Published by
Oolichan Books
P.O. Box 10, Lantzville
British Columbia, Canada
V0R 2H0

Printed in Canada by
Morriss Printing Company Limited
Victoria, British Columbia

for Steven and Shane

Acknowledgements

Earlier versions of "Murder" and "West Hampstead" appeared in *Canadian Fiction Magazine*. An earlier version of "Murder" also appeared in *94: Best Canadian Stories* (Oberon).

The author would also like to thank Barbara Klunder for the use of the cover image and Steven Whittaker for the author photo.

Contents

The Garden, The Cut

They aren't opposites, the garden and the cut. It's not about good and evil. I'm too smart to take that easy route, that breezy avenue where there's the sunny half of the street and the shadowed half and what you do is watch how all the world's traffic roars up to one side or the other.

But still. When I see the blood blooming out of his wrist, I know the red tide tugs everything with it, a little. And a little, and a little more, that's what finally makes us lie down, curl up, and say, I give already.

This is who I am: I have brown hair, I work in a library, and I'm forty years old. If you say I'm mousey, I say look closer. I've driven a few men wild on my pull-out couch. Only a few, because I'd rather be alone. My skirts fit well and I like my own company. I've read a lot. A lot of things, like politicians and phone sex, make me laugh.

This is what happened: I live in a one-room suite in a rooming house with a big back yard. To get to the back yard I have to pass the door of Nichola and Bill, and when I sit on the bench out there I look at their darkened square of window. I know them a little, as ex-alcoholic and alcoholic. She talks, he growls. She's going back to school; as far as he's concerned society is fucked. She talks to me about her English assignments; he called me one day while she was at school to say he was dying.

The funny thing was that I knocked when I got to the back of the house. A friend once told me I have an over-developed sense of privacy. Then I realized, and pushed the door open. I found him sitting on the pull-out couch, his wrist flowing. It was very quiet as his life leaked out of the cut. He started to cry a little, tell me he'd always been a good worker and now he couldn't anymore. His liver was bad and he was scared to die. He looked up at me out of yellow, yellow eyes, like the last puppy. There was a pile of embroidered linen on a side table, and I threw it over the crack in his wrist, shouting at him to hold it and not move; I told him to shut up even though he wasn't saying anything. I called the ambulance and they came in two minutes. For two minutes we just looked at each other, looked and looked.

Looking is touching. He touched me, he put his death all over me.

Then the blue suits were there, efficiently whisking everything into the back of the ambulance and shutting the doors on it. I didn't tell anyone about it. Whenever I thought I might, I'd look at the person I was going to tell, look at the person's crumpled collar or smell the person's human smell muffled in a cardigan, and think, what's the point? A badly-fitting suit, a too-eager smile, an attempted suicide, what's the difference? Would I be telling the person anything new? That's what I said to myself. Or maybe I was hugging the cut like a secret lover, mine.

I was working in the Juvenile section and noticed a book that shouldn't have been there. I took it out to move it, but I put it in my bag and brought it home. It was an exploitative New York-y thing, with watercolours and gothic textual splashes, about vampires. The watercolours suggested breasts and cocks and lots and lots of blood. Teeth in, ecstasy, death. I couldn't stop looking at the blood. I went to the store, bought some dye, and coloured my hair a deep red. I felt like the other woman.

Bill came back, Nichola told me, three days later. He was staying inside to recover. The window of the room where he was sleeping was small and dark and looked onto the back yard; the glass went from grey to black, every day. Nichola thanked me for being a friend and went in and out of the house with paper parcels, supplies for carrying on with life. It was spring and I wanted to make a garden. At least, I knew I had wanted to make gardens before, in the spring.

I didn't enjoy the digging that much. The problem was that I had no faith in the seeds, that they would grow. Why should they? Of course I knew that they would, because that's what always happens, but I just couldn't see the point of all that thrusting through the soil, all that becoming. Still, it was steadying to lean into the ritual turning of the clods, the repetition.

I stood at the beach once, with a sort of lover. We were looking at a rock just under the surface of the ocean, and on the rock gripped hundreds of limpets or something like that, small and crusty. Hundreds and hundreds. A thought came into my head, and I said, But what are they *for*, I said, what are they *for*? He was a theology student, earnest and bright, and he said, God must express Himself at every level of Being, from the highest to the lowest. I said, You mean Being's dance card is full? He smiled, full in my face, and said, Yes. Doesn't it get claustrophobic in there, I said, all that full, fat, wholesome Being? I can see, I said, why Lucifer wanted to make holes in it, rip it with nothingness, give us some room to breathe. Dara, he said. Sometimes he just said my name. He wasn't smug. The truth is he was something like beautiful. I put my nothing, my no, all over him, roughed him up with my mocking affection, and left him whole. When I said goodbye, he looked right at me and said, You should at least vote in the next election, you should at least vote.

By the end of the digging, I was tired. It was exhausting turning the soil with the grey eye of window on me and the seeds hard and dry in their packages, laid out on the bench in a row. Finally it was done, and the soil was prepared. I popped the seeds in their holes. They grew.

When the peas were a few inches high and the broccoli started to look like something to eat, Bill came outside. His brown hair was brushed neatly back from his face, and his denim clothes looked clean, even starched. He spoke to me, growled softly to me, keeping his body sideways from the front of me and my hands caked with dirt. He wouldn't do that to Nichola again, he said. He was scared and society was fucked. His liver was fucked. He was going back in the house for another drink, he said. But someday he'd surprise us all.

When the broccoli was big enough, I cut some for Nichola and Bill. Before I came outside, I put on the Hallelujah Chorus and opened the windows, so I could still hear it as I hacked through the green stems. Nichola came to her door and took the broccoli. She thanked me again for being a friend. I told her to help herself to peas, and she told me that Bill was in jail now for scrapping with a cop. Her long greying hair was up in a bun, and her face looked tired and relieved. It's only for a little while, she said. It's not life or anything.

I'm forty years old. I haven't voted and I haven't told anyone about the cut. My garden grows. I work at the library, and I'm kind to people who want help, even when they're looking for stupid books. I laugh about it in my mind, but it doesn't really make me happy. I still don't know what limpets are *for*. Maybe someday I'll surprise us all.

Gastly Medley

I was seventeen and smart and melancholy and the seventies were dying in a big steel city in Ontario. Truth be told, the place is still lodged in that decade, sidewalks hectic with shag haircuts and leather fringes. Anyway, the saying was that when you hit rock bottom you went to Gastly, a nearby town, the asshole of the region, the armpit of the county, etc., etc. Gastly was mostly rural with a little downtown where you could find beer, French fries, black rock Ts, and a concert ticket outlet for waiting overnight to get tickets to Led Zeppelin or Frankie Vallie. The spectre of the fifties lit up the place with a faint electric cruelty about which the seventies had nothing much to say; so greying pompadours and shags jigged side by side in the Legion hall on Saturday night right-night-to-fight dances. Sha boom sha boom, stairway to heaven, oh ya. So this is just my little medley about Gastly, and Blair who pretended he knew words to songs he didn't, and beautiful Nance with the blue, blue eyes rolled up to McPherson's like nothing I've ever seen even now all this time later, and I've seen an old hippie who *loved* a brown rat. (Don't ask me how I know.) Oh, and a bit about me and the time the hole opened in the sky.

At seventeen I lost my swain, my true love, my one and only, the light of my life, tra-la. So I went to Gastly. I didn't actually go live there, but I got a boyfriend from there for the summer and that was good enough for my purposes, which, by the way, I've never been too clear on. But it wasn't that self-destructive rites-of-passage thing that smart seventeen-year-old girls do, I know that. Blair wasn't the least bit abusive, except if you count buying me presents every few weeks because girls in Gastly expected it—a locket here, a shirt there. Never a pair of underwear, though underwear, from what I could gather, was what it was all about. His dad found a pair of panties left by Blair's girlfriend and displayed them proudly, flying the fuck flag. At least Blair could do something right. Chip off the old blockhead. Blair's Dad: a little red-eyed midget where his brain should have been, happy happy days, cheating on his wife in full view of his mute and raging son, hand on blonde thigh at the bar stool, king of the pool installers in Gastly, could lay a mean drainage pipe. Blair hate hate hated him, the biggest most everywhere Dad in the world for always and forever and will join him when he's done becoming him, in the happy hereafter where they're all dancin' to that jailhouse rock. But I'm getting off track. Not that there's much of a track anyway. Gastly could drop through the cracks of time, and the angels who keep history wouldn't make half a squawk.

This is one thing that happened: Blair took me over to his friend McPherson's house in the boonies one night. McPherson was truly his first name. It sounded odd and distinguished, and it was in a way because his parents named him after a two-four. McPherson Yellow Label was popular for a short time in Gastly around 1962. McPherson was also distinguished by a fabulous white-blonde shag, sky-blue eyes, and a physique that teetered in the perfect fleshly moment between sleek and hulkish. Another distinction: he was the most stunningly vacuous sixteen-year-old to ever suck the earth. I don't mean that he preferred sex and drugs to Ibsen and Bach. That's how it should be in sixteen-land. I mean that he didn't seem to prefer or not prefer anything at all. Not that he was a bored and boring lump either; he was as active as a lizard. His complexion bloomed robustly beneath his permanent tan, he never felt

17

ill or hung over, he was never irritable. He glided along accumulating snappy used cars and girls that had never been used, fresh as day. He was neither cocky nor humble—no sweaty anxiety either way. He wasn't stupid, just completely unruffled by thought or second thought. He ate, he drank, he slept. His pale, cool, emotionless greed fed on the world as silently as a maggot.

Oh yes, I said that something happened at McPherson's. We viewed a car. It was late at night on a Saturday about one or so, but all the bright white garage lights were on and McPherson's Dad and a few of his friends sat around on lawn chairs in the garage drinking beer. There was some low-key chuckling going on and a general sense of good-will, including approval of me (I looked good in my suede bomber jacket and tight jeans). And all this happy feeling was made possible by the souped-up repainted white sports car that gleamed at the centre of the garage. People weren't gaping at it in an unseemly fashion, just taking sidelong eye-sips as it hummed there silently throwing off waves of numinous light. The night was sufficient unto itself and there was no thought of the morrow.

"Nice mags," said Blair.

Another thing that happened: Blair took me to a mink farm at night. On the way he sang the songs on the radio, substituting syllables, not even whole words, for the lyrics he didn't know. There were actually a lot of things he didn't know, but he knew about minks and how vicious they were and how not to put your hands in the cages, just sticks. "There's a lady ha-nah all thor-on na is hah, and she's buying a stairway to heaven." Hum, hum, hum. We really didn't have a lot in common except vandalism, and we didn't even do that together. It was like parallel play: Blair, in smoky bars in Gastly, ripping down wall fixtures he wanted, I with my friend Minda, in that other city, nail-polish painting spanky new white cars we didn't want, under the cover of night and good reputations. Anyway, the minks were piled up in cages, bright white fur lozenges against the dark, but we didn't even get close enough to see if they were vicious or not because we parked the car and Blair opened the top he had given me and played with and tongued my breasts. This became our habit at the mink farm in Gastly. How was all that furrowing between my open buttons? The fact is, I don't really remember, but it wasn't like the lover and the two gazelles, for sure. I do remember the small scurrying sounds the minks made in their cages, though, like the night turning over in its restless, chilly sleep.

It was at an all-day bands go on-and-on thing on the outskirts of Gastly that I saw the hole in the sky. That was soon after Nance looked at McPherson.

Five of us piled into McPherson's pick-up to go

to the concert: me, Blair, McPherson, McPherson's girlfriend Nance, and Grub, McPherson's younger brother, who had none of McPherson's looks and even less of his luck. His good nature, however, held sturdy. Grub worked at a fish-and-chip shop doing all the worst, greasiest jobs for the lowest pay, but some excess happy gene somewhere kept his chunky cheeks smiling, and it wasn't a stupid smile either, it just kept breaking out all over his face. And he had his load to bear. Grub, himself, was actually in love with Nance and knew at some level that one day, quite soon, she would get fat and pregnant and tired and that he would love her even more and pat her hand reassuringly when she came home from the hamburger stand where she would work. They would be united in grease and dailyness. These were the dreams of the Grub.

But at the moment Nance was a truly blooming fourteen. I was in awe of her not so much for her flawless barely-out-of-babyhood face and corn-flower-blue eyes and silky calf-brown hair, but for how easily I would throw over my own cynical cat-egories for her. I thought that she was sweet and nice and lovely and all those things, and I thought this without a sneer. And she was, as the cliché goes, made for love. The cliché has it that it's like the flower turning to the sun, but with Nance the turn-ing itself was like light, and her soft body glowed that summer for McPherson, out to the ends of her hair. She was absolutely unselfconscious; there was not the tiniest posing in her love. Nothing to protect her from it, nothing at all. I'm still glad I wasn't around when McPherson moved on.

But the day of the concert I saw something worth seeing. We were all sitting in the grass in the sun, Blair mouthing some syllables along with the band doing a Cheap Trick cover, Grub eating French fries, and McPherson and Nance with their arms across each other's backs, huddled close, sometimes talking and laughing, sometimes watching the band.

And this one time when I looked over at them they had changed positions, Nance lying with her head in McPherson's lap and looking up at him and there really is nothing else in the universe. And there's nothing else for me but Nance looking up at McPherson, her eyes like blue planets in their still orbit of love. I see her profiled face, rapt against the sky, her clean, perfect devotion. I have never seen anything more holy. I don't like it, but there you go.

So why did the sky open? It did, though. The sun was just beginning to drop and the light was purpling. We were waiting for the next band and Blair was nattering about getting some dope. It was getting the slightest bit chilly. That's when I saw the hole, just a small gash, really, right above and to the left of the band shell. I knew what it meant. What it meant, for sure, was that I could never, never be fixed up inside. It seemed to me quite early in my young life for this to have happened, but it was clear that nothing could be done about it. The concert ended with a lame band, night fell, and some of us went to a mink farm, etc. etc.

It turned out that I was mostly wrong about the never never. Tra-la! But still, I just wanted to mention, along with those other things, the night when there was a hole in the sky. And it was chilly. And Blair was so dumb. And where was all this going, anyway?

Murder

I saw an old acquaintance yesterday, and he told me that another old acquaintance of ours had committed a murder out West. Vancouver he thought it was. So we had coffee at a grubby little restaurant on the unfashionable end of Queen Street where the ripped clothes are for real, and talked about Crane and the old days with Look Up. Since this acquaintance of mine didn't really have any important details about the murder, just that it had happened, our conversation was about the past. But now it was a past that oozed and quivered towards a ghostly present.

The Crane we talked about was already taking long strides up the stairs of a run-down rooming house in Vancouver, pale face garish in the dimly lit, narrow hall, moving towards . . . and there the movie cuts to black.

When I got home and the melodrama of our conversation faded, then I really started to think about Crane.

Look Up was an evangelical Christian group that had made its way into our high school through sports. The people who organized Look Up were mostly in their mid-twenties and offered themselves as coaches for athletic activities. They had attended the school themselves as teenagers and were actually good athletes, so the administation gladly took them on as alternatives to half-willing, saggy-assed history teachers. It turned out then, that if you were involved in sports, especially cross-country running or track and field, you were in some way involved in Look Up, even if it was only to eat the free hot dogs passed out at revival barbecues.

Look Up tried to promote its version of spiritual commitment, and there was a lot of energy poured into conversion. But for all the Bible studies, retreats, and group prayer, there was very little real spiritual vigilance. You just said that you accepted Christ as your Saviour and reached for another hot dog, and the Look Up leaders didn't worry about you. Meanwhile, you were a mess.

I imagine an expression on His face as he looked down over that swarming colony of confused teenagers, all fear and libido, some trying to cram the easy words about Heaven and Hell into their gaping hungers. He looks a bit like David McFadden thinking about Americans. It probably seemed to Him very funny and very sad, as it seems to me now, more funny and more sad as it recedes further and further into the past.

Crane, like me, was on the cross-country running team. I guess we were also core members of Look Up. I'm not sure how to describe the distinction between core and fringe members of the group, except to say that there was an intensity in the relationships between us that had little to do with either Look Up's paternal God, or our individual interests and backgrounds, or even our liking or disliking of each other. This was in the seventies; in the sixties we might have called ourselves seekers. Looking back, I see that Crane was the most lost, intense, neediest seeker of all, and I feel that I was really after all on the edge of Look Up, even of my own memories of that time. When Crane had his fall from grace, people didn't seem to realize, least of all the Look Up leaders, that it wasn't because he had ceased to be serious. Crane was deadly serious, more serious even than God or Jesus, who always seemed to be in a meeting.

But that fall is the third of the three pictures I want to show. I think that's all I want to do, show you three pictures of Crane that I saw, that I was part of, and one that I've imagined with help from the acquaintance I saw yesterday. So this isn't really a story, just a few pictures.

In the first one, everybody's at a track and field meet in Sudbury. Most of Sudbury is ugly, but we're at the pretty university with the famous rubber track, and the sun is shining and everyone is happy because some people from our team have already won ribbons. I'm happy because one of them is me, and because I'm thirteen and not too burdened yet by my sex, just nicely saddled, just enough so that I can go over, warm but not burning, to where seventeen-year-old Crane sits on the hillside psyching up for his race. He sits under a broadly striped red and orange Mexican poncho and does his psyching inside there. But somehow he sees me from underneath the thick material and puts his head out, and then takes off the poncho altogether. Leaning back on his arms he stretches his legs, and then grins. I notice everything about him at once. His limbs are long, but also thick and muscular; he has dark hair and ugly-beautiful thick features, square white teeth—a horselike charisma that attracts both sexes. I grin also, and am not embarassed by the fact that I see his testicles peeking out of his track shorts. It is simply a moment of mutual grinning. We're both warm, but not burning. It's very simple.

There's something else here, but I'm not sure if it's in the picture or not, because I didn't realize it at the time, only later. It makes the picture less warm and simple. The thing is that although I'm attracted to Crane, Crane is not attracted to himself. He feels ugly. That makes a lot of difference.

In the second picture it is late at night and a group of Look Up people are sitting around a fireplace in a log cabin in Haliburton. This is before my nominal conversion, my "witnessing," and I'm having a really good time with the wind howling outside and ten or twelve people all focussed on me, me, trying to get me to give myself to Him, to say I'll do it, to accept Him into my proud heart. All I have to do is say it, say that I'll accept Him as my Saviour. The drama is that I'm in the exquisite, lambent, holding-out stage, where Christ is really knocking like crazy and I'm leaning with my shoulder against the door, sort of trying to hold Him out but ready to surrender at any moment. I'm making all my academic objections, and they're countering with irrational truth. But really the whole drama is going on down below at some sexy level of sweaty wills and pushing and pulling, and really God is just waiting patiently somewhere for me to grow out of myself a little bit so that we can have a decent conversation.

In spite of my self-involvement in this picture, there is something that I see there about Crane, something that memory grasps in fits. Crane is one of the people in the group surrounding me near the fire. He plays his part as conversion vulture, but the whole time he is sending me messages, warning me away from conversion, as from death. I don't know how he does it, I can't remember what he says, how he gets it across while everyone is there, what words or signs he uses. The thing is like a smell or a taste, and I receive it. Did I receive it then? Or only now? Time is blurry, but the message is very clear. It comes from Crane not as from someone who has scorned the whole conversion thing, removed himself, intact, from it, but as from someone who's in it up to the neck, struggling in a fury of need and hunger, sorely infected by the sticky simplistic doctrines, neither healed by them nor able to escape them. The picture: Crane somehow saying to me, Don't do it, don't do it, not realizing, I guess, how much lower my stakes in it are; a year later I walked away from Look Up, and from my eventual "witnessing," without a look back, without a regret, without anger, without even a derisive chuckle. I just walked away into a different landscape. But now I see how high, how treacherously high, his stakes were. I don't know if I realized it then, or what I could have done with that realization, but now the picture moves back into the easier focus, and I just see me there, all these people trying to convert me, me ready to grant yes or no, toying, seductive, the centre.

The third picture is very straightforward. In it Crane strolls the halls of the high school, causing a bit of a stir. There is a leer on the big horsey features, and he acknowledges the stares he receives with a raunchy snort. He wears one of the familiar Look Up T-shirts, but with a difference: he has printed "Fuck" in front of the embossed felt lettering, so that the T-shirt now reads "Fuck Look Up." The whole thing is predictable. There is a contingent of the student body that reacts with delighted approval. Go, Crane, go. There are some students who find it distasteful, even though they have no particular affection for Look Up-ers. The Look Up leaders and core members are upset; they talk a lot about it, except to Crane, whose backsliding has taken a more unusual form than they are used to handling. In their typical blindness they fail to see that what they have in their midst is, though childishly expressed, a genuine spiritual event. I'd like to make my point by saying that at this period I once witnessed Crane crying in the stairwell of the school. But I never saw such a thing, and I doubt it ever happened. Yet my mind sees something real when it moves to a dark space where Crane's white face rages, fierce with tears.

Now for the picture that I imagine. My acquaintance told me the bare details yesterday in the restaurant on Queen Street. He was at a party about a year ago when he last saw Crane, just before Crane moved out to Vancouver. Simply, Crane told a group of guys at the party that he had fucked a blind man in the ass for money, and that he had laughed doing it. That's all. I don't imagine the actual blind man or the actual fucking, but the telling. Crane surrounded by a group of young men who want to listen to him, who hover around his musky dangerous presence, who take it seriously. Crane whiskey-drunk, but not so drunk (not ever) that he's letting things slip. He's squinting and sneering and laughing a blurry laugh, full of himself, at the centre, but he never loses sight of the faces of the men around him; he keeps his eye on every twitch and nuance, knows the effect of his power and watches it like a hawk. He starts the story of the blind man who touches him in the alley, and scans the group of young men with his perfected unwatchfulness for any signs of disapproval or disbelief. But no, he's got them, they're tense with gruesome excitement, blind and fuzzy with cigarette smoke and gin. He tells the story slowly: the sweat and the scornful sex and the pocketed fifty bucks, as the young men lean in closer and closer, and then finishes with an explosive jackal laugh, dizzy with hatred, sending the young men spinning into orbit but sure to come back, pulled by the gravity of his putrefaction.

And those are my pictures of Crane, the murderer.

I have something to confess. Crane didn't murder anyone, not that I know of. I guess he's still out West, or wherever, looking for whatever Easterners are always looking for out there. But when I think of that face, the grin still alive in it, and the Mexican poncho, and the innocent testicles, I think of murder. Fuck, fuck, fucked away at something until it was dead. Or tried to. He really threw it to himself, didn't he? Didn't you, Crane? Did you get rid of it that night, get rid of that difficult thing, that raw thing that still held you, mercifully, to your fierce grief? Did you? Did you fuck it all out? I'd really like to know. I really would.

Chairman Mao

In the late seventies my high-school teacher with
the flawless pageboy slammed me against the wall
because I missed last class and couldn't do the square
dance, the boy part, and she loved me and she hated
my new pot-smoking and too-bright boyfriend and
she, and all of us girls, and all the boys, and all the
other teachers maybe, we didn't have the foggiest
idea of where we were. In history, that is. Talkin'
'bout my generation. But that wasn't our generation. Ours was the next one, sneaking up on its pad-
ded earthshoed feet in ambush of . . . nothing.
Even though the sixties, and Vietnam, and student protests, and all that had already happened.
Even though the Beatles had sung "Revolution."

We were a vacant lot, nothing coming in and nothing going out.

Except for the penis of Mark Chapin, that is. It was going in and coming out of Jill Moyers, apparently, with all of Mark's friends looking in the Moyers' basement window. Jill was unconscious, dead drunk. Mark said to me at a party that he could do anything to Jill, anytime. Why did it matter?

Here's who we girls were: Marianne, who always looked up to the left (my right), Brenda—a twin, Jill—the other twin, Leslie, who could go to the high-school bathroom by herself, and me.

The night that Mark was going to do anything to Jill, I stepped outside with Marianne, and we rolled a car. You would have thought Leslie and I would make a better pair. We both had boyfriends, but we didn't finger them like worry beads. (No, that isn't true. We kept a few fingers for ourselves, that's all.) But it was Marianne that I was braced beside in the cold Hamilton street, our knees bent, flanked by tall boys, pushing and puffing, then standing back to watch the slow, satisfactory slide of car on ditch. It was no-one's car we knew. There was no reason to roll it. We had neither too much nor too little. (Unless you consider the whole, and we didn't.) We weren't sexually fondled as children. We weren't trying to change the world. We did well in school. The car was newish and white and hard, and we needed to ruin it. What did we think while we were rolling it? What did we say? All I remember is that we were cold.

We went back in to the party, held at whoever's house starred absent parents. On the stereo, Rush ambled through "Closer to the Heart," Neil Peart providing the plodding manic drums behind Geddy Lee's screeching about kings and re-al-i-ty. I took another beer from the fridge, and Mark Chapin passed me a toke. (I drank and smoked very little, with indifference.) Marianne was still beside me, and beside her was her boyfriend Mitch. Mine was somewhere else in the house.

"Still at Shell?" I asked Mitch.

"Yep. Thirty hours a week now. After school, nights, weekends."

"Going to Mac next year?"

"I'm starting in January. Going into Business."

"Right. Good program for getting a job." I threw in, for a joke, "Who's the premier of Ontario, Mitch?"

"Don't know. What's it matter?"

"Don't know either," I said. I didn't.

We were fairly industrious. Most of us did our homework, most of the time, and a lot of us had jobs. We didn't expect not to get jobs in the future, if we thought about it. We didn't think about it. In this, our last year of high school, I wrote a prize-winning essay on eating images in *Pincher Martin*. The novel is a mind-walk about a guy on an island

34

who stews in his own juices. I'd never read a whole newspaper. I didn't know of anyone who had.

Marianne wanted to go to the bathroom, so we went after she unpeeled Mitch's hand from her waist. She was getting thinner every day. She'd told me that she thought skinny women with big breasts were more appealing. More than what? I thought, but didn't ask. We weren't that close, except for our common habit of destruction. Marianne sat on the toilet and looked up to the left.

"Brenda and Jill are sharing a brain again," she said. "Jill's been seeing Mark Chapin. She told me he wrote her a song and played it on his guitar. He's going to her house after the party." Marianne snorted. She finished, zipped up her pants, and went to the sink. She brushed her hair and went out.

On the way back to the living room, we passed the kitchen, where a cake was being scooped into by everybody's hands. I reached in and grabbed a piece, gobbled it. Marianne didn't touch it, snaking her body away from the kitchen as she passed and clamping her face shut. Her furious intelligence squeezed itself tighter and tighter, a cobra between whose coils no food could sneak.

I sat on the couch beside Mark Chapin. He was going to be painting in the summer and then take off to university in a city a few hours away. Once a few years ago we'd had an argument because I spilled a sticky drink on his jacket at a formal dance. He wanted me to pay for the jacket's cleaning. I remembered thinking that it was such an adult thing to want, but I didn't pay for it. We had no further arguments.

There was talk, smoke, chat. About not much. Somewhere in the buzz Mark turned to me and whispered softly.

"I'm seeing Jill," he said, and looked at me.

"I know," I said.

"What do you think?" he said. He had very black eyes and was cultivating a small, almost pointed beard.

"Not much. What do you think?"

Suddenly we seemed alone, in our private theatre. The background noise was the stage and out came Mark to give me a performance, a glistening after-hours walk-on. His voice was vicious and high; he mimicked the twisting of hair around a finger.

"That's neat, that's so-o-o neat!" Over and over.

I was stunned into simplicity.

"You're imitating Jill."

"No," he said. "If I was imitating Jill, I'd do this." His face assumed a dopey loll, tongue thick, eyes glazed. But the black at their centres was pure, overproof hatred.

I watched the performance like I read Burroughs later, shocked by its cruelty but not really *believing* in it. It was hard to believe in anything in Hamilton, Ontario, in 1979. Not even when Jill's twin

36

Brenda told us the next day about the scene with Mark and Jill in the basement and the boys in the window. I don't know how she knew: Brenda was asleep herself, she said. Jill was unconscious, or was it almost? I don't remember.

I heard "Revolution" recently in the Dairy Queen, from the machine. I sat with my son, who was eating his ice cream, put in my quarter and watched the quaint record go under the needle. "You say you want a rev-o-lution, we-ell you know, we all want to change the world." Rocking horse energy gallop, young strong male voices in the saddle. What a conscious party.

And then, "But if you go carryin' pictures of Chairman Mao/ You ain't gonna make it with anyone anyhow." More waterfall energy, cascading over the edge of the drums, "Don't you know it's gonna be . . . ALRIGHT!
be . . . ALRIGHT !"

So, was the sixties all about makin' it with anyone anyhow? Revolution with no strings? Maybe the strings were like kite ribbons, decorations slapping the breeze, so pretty, prettier than kings and re-al-i-ty. A kite without a tether, the ribbons waving like long hair, the main line held by no one?
Don't know.

Valerie

I met Valerie when I was in England one summer taking a few months off from my real life in Canada. We would stay up late talking in the lobby of the student residence where we were living, or during the day go out walking the streets of London under the rare bright sunshine that graced the city that year. We had an easy companionship, moving without awkwardness from gossip about the other students in the residence to details of our own small pasts. For topics, there were literature, men, sex and food, our four pillars. We ate fried onion rings in a tiny park in Soho while talking about these things, and posed for each other. We modelled our commitments and carelessnesses with the same loose panache, each strolling in the other's runway mind. We told stories, expecting—always—exquisite bibelots. We shared a horror of the ordinary.

We were, too, physical presences to each other. I gather from things she said and a poem she wrote me that I left Valerie with an impression of smallness, featheriness and lightness, with streaks of purple shadow at the eyes. Tall and dark, with wavy jet black hair cut in aggressive angles about her ears, Valerie existed for me most forcefully in the way she pronounced the "l"s in consonant groups separately. "Black" thus became "be-l-ack." This linguistic habit had the same sensual and disturbing effect on me as the fragrance patchouli, which I first smelled that same summer in the arms of a seedy drummer on the top of the Roman wall surrounding York. At least a few times every summer since, I stand at a particular Indian vendor's table on Yonge Street and sniff at a little glass bottle of the oil. I still don't know if I like it or not.

She is bits of memory now. This Valerie made me love shoes. She introduced me to Robert Haas' "Meditations at Lagunitas," a poem I still read with keen pleasure. (It has be-l-ackberries in it.) She liked the long skinny knit skirts just coming out in London then, in the mid-eighties, and adored her father, a well-known social historian living in Chicago. She admired but felt unsuited to monogamy. Had had a nice Swede for her birthday, the week before I arrived at the residence. Would not hurt her parents by living with a man, though, not married. At a reggae festival in an English park, I asked her if she thought we acted, fundamentally, out of rejecting or embracing things—people, ideas—and she said (moving sleepy hips to "Rebel Music") they were part of one process. We asked each other questions like that often, and they seemed to mean something at the time.

We became friends when she was sitting on the front steps of the residence and I was jogging by. We had already had a few words at the pub, and in the cafeteria over a watery mess of what passes for *aubergine* in England. She made fun of my jogging shorts, too retro seventies I think. I shot back that she could shove a brisket of Terry's New York corn beef up her ass. Terry was a fellow student who had whined his way through the summer, pining for the United States and living only to receive packages of meat from his parents. I knew Valerie hated him, would eat the meat he slathered with mustard and so enthusiastically shared with us, and then in the pubs do imitations of his cringing.

I sat down, in my shorts, beside her on the front steps.

"You know," she said, "by this point you're the only person in the whole residence I like." I knew she wasn't kidding.

"I feel the same," I said. "It's because we don't know each other."

"Ooh, ugly truths about human nature on a sunny day in a world-class city, home to great paintings and really old books. Do you know that they have Jeremy Bentham's penis in a jar at the University?"

Valerie told me a lot about her life and family back home in the States, but the most mythologized character in her private theatre was a young man named Robert Epstein. Epstein was, apparently, brilliant and morose. Valerie had fallen in love with him at that dangerous age when she, herself so brilliant and morose, read Kierkegaard and found tortured people devastatingly attractive. What Valerie failed to realize at the time, she said, was that Epstein was *really* morose, so morose, in fact, that he decided to spend the rest of his life working in a submarine for the government. She had written and still wrote him letters down there, but no reply had broken the surface of his violently calm, perfect fuck-you to life. She managed to make all of this into an amusing story for me, a jaunty narrative. But I knew it still had power in her life, unwinding in her blood, slowly, like a time-released virus.

A young man in our residence, himself a Londoner, gradually and insistently began to assume the king bee position in our student hive that summer. Tall and blonde, with a cool blue stare, Andrew towered above all the other men in the residence in looks and charm. I grew to despise him with an intense and almost physical hatred. His reptilian detachment and huge arrogance were fascinating. There was a savage forgetfulness about him; he managed to dodge all questions about his family and his past in polite, well-oiled verbal dekes that were truly mysterious to me. Even though he looked directly at people when he talked to them, there was always the sense that his gaze was sliding off into another place.

Many women wanted to sleep with him, and did. Later he would make casually insulting remarks about them to other women. This had its aphrodisiac effect on the untried women, who promptly took their places outside his bedroom door. He imitated one woman from Quebec, "Please Andrew, I have such a need, such a need!" rubbing his hands underneath where his breasts would be, rolling up his blue eye-stones in feigned helplessness. I imagined that he took his pleasures like cocktails, laying hold of them with the measured, slightly bored reach of the whiskered Old Boy by the fire at his Club.

Once, in a hallway, he drew two fingers over my wrist, and spoke with cryptic purpose.

"You're the one, at the end of it all."

He, or I, walked away.

One day on one of our onion ring excursions, Valerie mentioned that she and Andrew had been spending quite a lot of time together recently. Her taut mouth almost but not quite resisted dissolving into a soft poached smile when she told me that he was incredibly strange and interesting. I thought for a moment and then distilled my displeasure into what I thought was a polite, but pointed question.

"Does he really exist? When you talk to him, does he exist in the same moment with you?"

Valerie was not at all surprised by my question and answered it quickly and fervently, as if she had given the matter a lot of thought already.

"Yes, I really think he does. I really do." She paused and pulled at some grass where we were sitting. "But I'm not sure if he exists from moment *to* moment. That's what I'm trying to figure out now." She looked up at me a bit shyly and defensively, as if sure she was on the trail of something of mammoth importance but afraid it wouldn't meet with the reverence it deserved in the civilian world. I hated to see her like this.

"Fascinating research, I'm sure," I said, feeling immediate shame for my cheap and unimaginative sarcasm. I pulled my sweater closed.

The conversation drifted away to other things. We talked for a while about the lecturers we'd heard that morning and about the course director with his fixation on Pope. (Dr. Smythe had been whacking away for twenty years on a dissertation titled "Alexander Pope and the Uncoupled Couplet." We were young enough to be more amused than disgusted.) But even our imitations of Dr. Smythe stretching his teeth over "What is, is RIGHT" were without energy. The afternoon was not turning out well at all, was not a bibelot. Soon we fell into silence and watched a line of children in the park tagging along behind their teacher and holding onto a long thick rope. A little boy fell down and hurt his knee, and was right away being comforted by the teacher and a sympathetic flock of little girls who warmed him back into cheerfulness with their attention.

The afternoon was drowsing to a close and neither of us had spoken for a while. I broke the silence first.

"I bet he even has a cold John Thomas," I said, affecting both jauntiness and an English accent.

"Who?"

"Your pal Lucifer."

"I'm surprised at you. You're not usually so judgemental. So ke-l-osed to possibility."

"I can't imagine him asleep. I don't like that."

No answer.

"Well, I guess if there's a mountain, you gotta climb it. Or mount it."

I didn't see much of Valerie for a few weeks.

One Saturday night, near the end of it all, there was a party in someone's room in the residence. I was missing a man back in Toronto, and I drank a lot. Most people did drink for one reason or another. Our course was over, and the air was stuffy with attractions, resentments big and small, woozy sentimentality and ambition, all out of the box. I had drawn a lightning bolt at the corner of my eye with eyeliner, and everyone wanted to take a picture of me. Someone said I looked like the model Edie someone-or-other. I nearly lost consciousness because I didn't take it seriously when the cute couple from Alabama told me not to swallow the tobacco juice, just spit it out. Terry told me he loved me, and I told him he was gay. (I got a letter years later, thanking me for this insight.) It was a wonderful and nauseating party. Finally, I had to go to the bathroom.

Making my way very cautiously down the hallway, holding out one seasick hand against the wall, I managed to find the right doorway. I passed through it and went immediately to the sink, where I turned on the cold water tap and splashed my face. I ran water over my wrists. Sometime during these difficult operations, I noticed that I had not noticed something. I tried to focus, at first without success. Drying my face, I found I needed to sit, sit, sit, if I were to be conscious.

It was then I heard the absence of the sounds I had not fully registered when I came in the bathroom. Something had stopped, was in limbo. My groggy mind made a quantum leap, and I looked over to the single toilet cubicle in the room, where four feet stood, hushed, waiting for me to go away. Two of the feet were Valerie's; I recognized the shoes from the pile of assorted garments strewn around the floor of the little cubicle. Andrew's expensively casual garments completed this crazy salad. I remember being faintly surprised that they weren't folded.

They could have used her room, or his. They didn't.

Soon whispers were coming from the cubicle, sounds I heard as tactful invitations to the intruder, me, to exit stage left. (Did I hear well?) I would have been so glad to leave, but found to my humiliation that my legs wouldn't work. In an absurd gesture of modesty I turned my eyes away from the cubicle towards the opposite wall, remaining rooted to the floor while my head spun. I silently mouthed "want," "jealous," and "undone," over and over, but they seemed like words in another language that didn't translate well. And then, for a long time, I leaned with my face against the hard cool porcelain of the sink and thought how the sounds of love in a bathroom bore a striking resemblance to the surreal and hollow echoing inside a submarine.

West Hampstead

West Hampstead is not Hampstead. Such is the power of names that I assumed at some gut level that the former would bear some resemblance to the latter, with its elegant narrow streets and Keats' death held respectfully in his tree-shadowed house. I had seen Hampstead earlier in the summer when I was at the University of London, and had loved it. West Hampstead, surely, would be a good place to spend the last four days of my trip before returning home to real life in Canada.

I had travelled that summer up and down the British Isles and been more or less comfortable in the hostels and bed-and-breakfasts I stayed in. I was sometimes lonely, sometimes high, but almost never scared. I had brushed danger softly a few times, a pungent and silky black tulip. I began to foster an image of myself as a small but tough surveyor of life. Perhaps such strut demanded that England roll over and turn up its underbelly at parting.

I knew the moment I walked up the short path to the West Hampstead Youth Villa that it was not a nice, maybe not even a decent, place. It was a Victorian house on the outskirts of town, obviously once impressive. Like so many others on this sad street it had long ago lost its dignity, with no one to care for it, and was year by year settling more dejectedly into the weedy ground it sat on. But with few pounds in my pocket and four days to stretch them across I couldn't afford to be selective. My travel book, so far fairly reliable, described this place as unspectacular but cheap.

The front door was open, so I walked in and stood for a moment in the musty hall painted that evil shade of turquoise that seems always and only to accentuate squalor. A genderless person wearing tights made out of a British flag emerged from an adjoining hallway, looked at me with sloe-eyed disinterest from under a mop of laboriously ruined hair, and disappeared into a crevice somewhere before I could say a word. My first instinct was to turn around and leave, but I didn't want to be middle class in front of myself.

I found the check-in office. There, the bedraggled staff lounged thinly on desk tops and chairs. I could not see individuals at first but only a crazy salad of waxy yellow complexions, greasy locks of hair, skinny arms and legs sticking out of tattered bits of clothing, and an alarming number of absent teeth. In a flash of lucid, emotionless knowing it became clear to me that all of these half dozen or so people were addicts of some kind, possibly heroin.

At first there was no exchange at all. The people in the room looked at me incuriously, with unblinking glances that seemed to slide off into some universe parallel to mine, near but infinitely distant. Finally I said to anyone listening that I wanted a room for three nights and asked what it would cost. A tall man wiping lanky brown hair out of his eyes moved towards a desk and dragged his hands over some papers. He couldn't seem to find what he wanted, but this didn't increase the speed or vigour of his search. He looked up.

"Single room?" he asked, in a thick garbled accent I didn't know.

When I answered yes, his hands went back to their useless trawling. I didn't understand why he needed to look through papers to quote me a price, and he decided at last that he didn't either.

"Six pounds thirty-five a night," he said, looking up. He spoke with a deep rich lisp, and his mouth twisted, uncomfortable with the passage of words.

I could feel the eyes of the others upon me as he quoted his price, but strangely, I didn't have the usual sense of shrewd glances being exchanged, only a kind of stunted gaming interest.

"Five pounds," I countered, feeling foolish (I hated to barter), but guessing that this was expected. The room was silent with dull watching while the scraggly leader deliberated.

"Six pounds."

"Fine." And for no reason at all, I paid him for the three full nights up front, though this was neither asked for nor expected.

After I had paid, one of the women took me up to my room. She was extremely thin but her arms and legs looked as if they might have once possessed some wiry strength. She wore a sleeveless A-line dress of a faded material popular two decades or so before. Her hair was short and stiff, sticking out like chicken feathers around her face.

"There you are dear," she announced as we arrived at a dingy room on the top floor of the house. I turned around to thank and dismiss her and found that she was watching me with a maternal expression, almost grotesque in her greyish mask of a face. I didn't know what to say so I trotted out my usual traveller's question, "Do you like it here?"

I saw at once from the woman's expression that she didn't understand. Her gaze made a brief circuit around the room, up to the ceiling, down to the baseboards, then out to the hall.

"I live here," she said finally with an already wilted half-smile, hoping she had pleased me. I tried to look appreciative and then shut the door gently but firmly, vaguely ashamed yet relieved to close out that tragic gash in the woman's face where the attempted smile had been.

"Thank you!" I yelled out from behind the door and heard her slowly descend the stairs.

The room was actually quite large as bed-and-breakfast rooms go, but there was only one very tiny window, overlooking the street. There was also a dirty sink, a chest of drawers, a closet, and a bed that, I knew from just looking, was musty and permanently damp. So was the thin pinkish rug that crawled across the floor. An old Marianne Faithfull poster, so washed out it was almost sepia, decorated one wall. I could already imagine horrible things happening there, baroque spasms of violence or need, under Marianne's drugged and fading stare. My thought was not to look too closely at anything.

Going over to put my things on the bed, I became aware of an unmistakable odour, a rude presence flapping darkly around the edges of my mind. I decided to ignore it at first.

After sitting on my bed for a few minutes, I managed to laugh a little at my situation, trying to look at it from a bird's eye or perhaps future perspective. What a glorious way to end this trip, a trip that had really begun in Canterbury Cathedral where I had hovered in unusual stillness over Thomas à Becket's tiny candle—drawn there day after day, a twentieth-century moth discovering an enormous hunger in its tiny body. Then the series of others—Salisbury, York, Ely, Coventry—each shaping the silence in different leapings of stone and light. And at the end of it all, I had touched down here, on this particular mound of dirt.

I could no longer ignore the smell and soon found its source in a wet patch of rug to one side of the door. Looking at the stain, I realized that it was actually coming from somewhere just outside the base of the wall. I opened my door, peered around, and saw another door that I had not noticed before when the grey-faced woman led me up the stairs. Puzzled because I had thought mine was the only room for let on this floor, I edged the door open and discovered a tiny filthy cubby hole with a toilet and sink.

I peered into the toilet. "This toilet has not been flushed since the dawn of man," I said out loud. Fear was already ballooning like some malignant yeast, feeding unwillingly but with appetite on this ugly banquet.

But then I reasoned—what was this after all but a toilet filled with piss (smelling, so what, of gin) and shit, seeping its contents onto the floor, under the door, and into my room? What, really, was the threat? It called for disgust, maybe, but hardly terror. Where was all that stupid terror coming from?

I sat on my bed and tried to read. I couldn't concentrate so I decided to go out and explore West Hampstead. I was about to walk out when I realized that I wanted to take my things, all of them, with me. I chastised myself for this bit of paranoia, but couldn't get out of my head the image of the grey-faced woman wearing one of my funky Soho dresses, the sleeves hanging limply on her scarecrow's body; I saw her wolfing down the marmalade I had bought at Harrod's for the friend of an aunt. She obviously hardly ate, I said to myself, and what did it matter if she wore my dress? But I took all of the things anyway.

Lugging my backpack over my shoulder, I went out into the late afternoon sunshine. The centre of town with its many old trees and red roofs pointing up into the soft light seemed almost charming when I had been out for a while, and I began to speculate that West Hampstead Youth Villa, or perhaps the area of town it was in, was only a smudge on an otherwise healthy complexion. But after trekking around, I realized that it was again a matter of not looking too closely at things. The streets were grimy, the shops mostly in a state of disrepair, and many of the faces bedevilled by something like want. I saw a woman take a pear from a fruit stand. The fat yellow curve of the pear dropped from the expert clutch into her bag without a fuss.

After a few hours of walking I rested in a parkette that bordered a school. Thinking, I guess, that grass is soft everywhere, I set my things down and, using my pack as a pillow, stretched out on the turf under the shade of a tree. For a while I simply lay there listening to the hum of my blood.

I was just beginning to uncoil when something that was at once familiar and strange assaulted my senses. I sat up rigidly with the uncanny impression that the stench of my room had followed me. I don't know whether I was more relieved or disgusted when I realized that the source of the sweet-slop odour of excrement was not my fetid brain, but real dog shit deposited liberally around the edge of the park. Lots of flies were in noisy attendance, their heavy dark bodies tumbling in drowsy ecstasy over their treasure.

There was nowhere for me to go. And so I went back.

When I returned from the shit-and-flies park, I once again sat on my ever-damp bed with my things beside me and gazed around the room. I would not unpack. Only too well could I imagine myself opening the ruined chest of drawers and finding some horror-show there (animal? mineral? vegetable?) that would turn the screw on my already painful state of watchfulness. I tried to relax, breathe deeply, but my nerves never stopped buzzing. I realized that an hour had passed and I had not moved. My eyes were dry with watching.

Just as I was considering the possibility of going out again, the door opened and one of the shades entered, this one a woman with long colourless hair and the shuffling gait of the aged, though she was probably no more than thirty-five. When she saw me, her face registered a stunted, gradual surprise.

"Oh, you're at home dear!"

Hardly, I thought. But before I had a chance to ask what she was doing in my room at that hour, she whisked her thin body from the door as fast as a cockroach. Soon she appeared with a tattered grey rag and a canister of scrubbing powder.

"Sink needs a quick wipe," she said, approaching the basin with renewed listlessness. I looked at my watch: quarter past eight in the evening.

The woman took a few half-hearted swipes at the inside of the sink and then dragged the soggy cloth around the faucets. Neither she nor I said anything while she worked.

"That'll do nicely then," she said finally, with an alarming black-toothed grin in my direction. In a sudden begrimed flash of imagination I saw a large flake of the woman's yellow skin peel itself from her face and make a long, slow drift towards the floor, where it settled in a patch of late sunlight, a messenger from some jangly, hellish autumn. Then she turned and ambled through the door, and I was alone.

I stewed on my bed for a while, still unmoving, coming to the decision not to go out. I didn't want to carry my things again, and the prospect of foraying into the West Hampstead night in search of a clean, well-lighted place was hardly cheering. I would stand my ground, defending my grungy territory with senses alert.

An hour or so later I had just begun to settle into *A Handful of Dust* when a light tap on the door sent shock waves through me.

"Who is it?" I yelled. There was silence for a moment, and then a muffled reply that I couldn't make out.

"Who's there?" I said, and found that my hand had been searching through my bag for a tiny pocket knife I carried. There were some shuffling noises outside the door, and then more silence. Finally the reply came: "Cleaning staff."

After a few more moments of waiting on both sides, the knocker pushed open the door. It was the tall man who had let me the room, grey cloth and cleaning powder in hand. Nearly giving way to truly hysterical laughter, I loudly and firmly declared that the sink had already been cleaned, thank you, and good night. The lanky person walked towards the basin, looked in, and furrowed his brow.

"I'll not be sayin' that's clean, will you?" His brogue was thickly certain.

I found myself in the absurd position of having to agree.

"I'll just give it a quick wipe and you'll feel more comfortable," he said, dragging the cloth around the basin.

Watching, entranced, the soulless sweeping motions of my host, I realized several things at once. I suddenly knew that were I to get up, approach him, and stick my knife into his side, it would go in with fearful ease, his knees would bend from under him and he would crumple up into a heap without a struggle or a word. And I also knew that the people in this house were unspeakably dangerous. The silent whine of evil was deafening.

"That's better," he said, swishing the cloth around one last time for good measure. Outside, the light was beginning to fade. My hand with the knife rested under the corner of the rumpled blanket I had wrapped around me.

"Incompetence," the man mumbled suddenly. "That's what I don't like. He mused for a moment, trying it on for size, and then said, "That's why I left Scotland. They wouldn't make the loaves properly there." Noticing me briefly, he added, "I was a baker once."

"What do you mean about the loaves?" I asked, playing my lunatic part in this new drama, still feeling my knife under the blanket.

He thought for a moment, his brow creasing with the effort of concentration and some ancient grievance.

"A loaf is like a life, I used to say. It has to go through a process. All of the parts, one at a time, and not before." He gestured in a laboured manner, as if underwater, his thin arms bobbing and stretching with a will of their own. "Not before." It was all so difficult. "Patience is a virtue," he concluded with something like exasperation.

As he spoke, the words emerging from his wrecked bony face, I had a glimpse of an atrophied artistic pride, floating around, still decaying, detached from a larger life. I looked away, as from a fish sputtering out its last life on the bottom of a boat.

"It rises up . . . up . . . up and then right away the Scots want to bring it down . . . down (grief-stricken look, fist pummelling the air to demonstrate Scottish brutality) before it's ready to be kneaded." He paused to wipe his lips. "And then they won't knead it properly. They don't bother. They rush. More loaves, faster, faster. It's insane . . . so I got away from it . . . what else (fatalistic shrug) could I do?"

Unable to find what he seemed to be casting about for, the ex-Scottish baker heroin addict with Ajax on his hands in my room collapsed into himself. It was nearly dark outside.

". . . it needs care . . . all the steps . . . kneading,

kneading, kneading . . . mmm . . . soft kneading . . .
she had sharp eyes though, that one, was always
watching . . . she said I was weak, she said that she
knew me, saw what I was . . . I couldn't help it that
night, there were so many people around, and lights,
and they brought it with them, yes they had it right
there in the room . . . I can't remember how it happened, how I got it on, squeezed it on, but there it
was . . . it was so cold when I came back . . . her eyes
were so green . . . ah, she *was* unkind to me, just so
unkind, and it was cold in the kitchen with the fire
in the grate gone out . . ."

There was silence for a few moments with the
dark opaquing the tiny window, my host staring
ahead into a past that would never quite focus, and
me wondering when I was ever going to get home.

"Thank you and good night," I found myself saying firmly, trying to stuff back into their box the
thin blacknesses winging around the room. The ex-
baker hardly heard me, I'm sure, but soon began to
collect his things and shuffle out, his blank expression suggesting that it was all going.

"Good night," I said again.

"Oh, yes, good night," he replied, just then reminded of, and at the same moment forgetting, my
existence.

Reflection crowded out fear, and soon I began to
feel sleepy. I debated briefly with myself about al-
lowing any lapse in watchfulness, but reasoned that

I would need some sleep if I were to be here three more days. I relaxed some, even as I instinctively turned my face away from the pillowcase, which was damp and sour.

In my dream the small plump child kept coming and coming at me, even though I pushed her away every time, each time with greater force. She was pale and soft in a frilly pink dress, with light brown curls and a hideous fat-cheeked sweetness in her expression. It was not gentleness or long-suffering.

The first time, she came up and wanted to sit on my lap and I didn't resist her, though the lack of any tautness in her face repelled me greatly. Crawling up into my lap, her soft, slightly damp skin brushing mine, she nestled her head of silk curls into the crook of my neck, settling there as if forever. I tolerated this with pity and fear.

Before I understood what was happening, I had a gagging sense of invasion. In a flash of knowing and seeing at once I realized the child's lily-white, humid little hand had entered my mouth somehow and that she was pushing her arm down my throat with soft but eager gurgles of satisfaction. I could feel the tiny hand grasping orgiastically and knew with clear terror that she would seize and take me if I let her. Already her little clawless fingers were curling around my secret heart, tickling it with their softness.

In a frenzy of revulsion and fear, I grasped her by the throat and thrust her from me, wrenching her arm from my ravaged inside. More terrifying than anything was this pallid creature's lack of resistance as my fingers pressed into the pillowy flesh of her neck.

But she kept coming. Slowly but surely toddling towards me on fat little legs, her expression unnaturally sweet and charmless. Every time she reached me, I would push her away, sometimes quite a distance, but she would always return. She never gained in strength and so never managed to invade me as she had the first time, but I realized with horror that I was her prisoner forever. I could never sleep or relax or become absorbed in any other thing. I must always be watchful. I must always push her away and she always come back, my pushing and her toddling an eternal souped-up game of swing. Unless I wearied, and then she had me. And already I could feel myself tiring, and hot and irritable with the fear of tiring.

I believe that I awoke with the very first, tiniest sound of the key in my lock.

"Get out!" I bellowed, and bolted upright. My door slammed shut and there was the sound of muffled voices and of feet stampeding down the staircase to the main floor. Then silence.

My mind opened like a jack knife: I had just frightened some people away from my door. Those people had tried to get into my room. No one in the whole world, except those people, knew where I was.

What to do became very clear. I would hold an all-night vigil and leave first thing in the morning. I had next to no money, but I would sleep and live in the airport on the floor for three days if necessary. There was nothing to do now but turn on my tiny reading lamp and wait.

The first little while passed without event. I simply perched, stiff with watching, on my bed and listened to the noises of parties going on in the houses up and down the street. I guessed from the extreme stillness of the house that my hosts and many of the people staying at West Hampstead Youth Villa were out there. Someone with hard-heeled boots kept crossing and re-crossing the street. I thought it might be the ex-Scottish baker.

From what I could make out, he was mumbling suggestions to the others with him, suggestions about coming, going, taking, leaving, seeing, and getting. But putting a feeler out into the blackness, I sensed that not much of this was getting done, though a lot probably happened to that motley crew in the corners of the night.

While the night wore on, the aimless echoing of those boots seemed to me more and more ghastly, a tinny shade of music from some underworld carnival.

As I cast about the room in a zombie-like circuit from one increasingly familiar mangy object to the next, I had a sense of something catching in my mind but not quite sticking. I did not want it to stick. A slow terror began to buzz in my veins, but in some instinct of perversity or truth I inched forward. I could not see it clearly, but I did see something truly horrific: I realized that I had known about it all along, from the moment I walked into this house. I had walked in here with my eyes, some eyes somewhere, wide open.

Uncurling from my stiff posture on the bed, I put out one foot and then the other, and rose. Thought had vanished. I moved towards what I had to see. Had to.

Sidestepping the wet patch on the floor and pushing the door open, I peered out into the hallway, which was lit by a series of uncovered dim bulbs. No one stirred. The house ached with silence. I passed quickly down the hallway, again pausing to listen. Nothing. My feet went numb as I descended the stairs, quickly at first and then more slowly as I neared the bottom.

To the left was the room where I had registered. Its door was open. I looked inside and saw no one. All along the lower corridor were closed doors, probably guest rooms. Nothing stirred. Where to go, now?

Turning my head, I noticed at the end of the lower hallway a door with a glass panel in its upper half. The glass glowed with a greenish light. I stepped quickly down the hallway and paused at the door, gathering nerve. This must be it.

When I pushed it open, I was surprised to find absolutely nothing. It was the emptiest room I had ever seen. I had thought of things—of flaps of neck flesh, of oozing filth or pleasure, of the sudden vacuum-suck into cool, weightless float. But not this characterless space. In so far as the room could be described at all, it could only be said to be large, greenish, and very, very empty.

Until I noticed in one corner of the floor a squar-ish opening, about two by three feet, with stairs going down. It was underground, of course.

Nerves stinging, I squeezed myself through the small opening in the floor and began the descent into this musty passage. My terror increased as my shoulders, neck and finally head passed below ground level into the darkness under the floor.

When my feet told me I had reached the bottom of the staircase, I rested for a few moments while my eyes adjusted to the very dim greenish light that hung damp and thick in the tiny room where I found myself. Looking around, I was unable to discern the source of the light, for once again, there was noth-ing in the room. Nothing to attack, nothing to run from. I stood there in my long nightshirt, in the sourceless dreamy light. My fear settled a little. This was only an unused root cellar of some kind.

Then I saw a low hatch in the side of the wall

closest to me. The little door was made of rotted wood, with its yellowish paint blistering and hinges rusted.

It must be inside.

Moving forward slowly with hands outstretched as if to ward off a sudden tempest of evil from within, I crouched down to eye-level with the door and then waited, listening. Nothing. My fingers tingled as I touched the rusty handle and then slowly pulled open the creaking hatch.

At first there was only darkness, and then the darkness took shape as a long, narrow corridor, barely large enough for me to wriggle along. The corridor, made of what looked like packed earth, went ahead into blackness forever. It had a slight medicinal smell, but other than that did not reveal itself. Overwhelmed with fresh fear and accumulated fatigue, I knew that I would have to go on. I knew it was in there. I put my head inside the tiny door-frame and began to inch forward.

I think it was the sunlight pouring through my tiny window that woke me up.

It was morning.

Extraordinarily bright sunbeams glancing off the objects in the room lent even the orphaned sink a small cheerfulness. I suspected from the noises I began to hear downstairs and from the new, tantalizing smells that were flooding up, even to this room, that breakfast was in the works.

Still, I knew exactly what I was about as I washed my hair, carefully made up my eyes, dressed, chose matching earrings, and packed neatly the few things I had taken out of my bag.

When I reached the lower floor, everything was as I had imagined. The obligatory breakfast was being made and the shades were up and about, the sunshine having shot up even their dreary frames with some of its life. The ex-Scottish baker was at the check-in table, moving around some papers.

"I want two nights' fees back. Some people tried to get into my room last night. They had a key. I'm not staying here." I was surprised by my own firmness. I had always hated confrontations over money.

The man registered no surprise, but the unexpected request wrinkled his brow some on this sunny delightful morning.

"We'll give you another room, Room Five on the lower floor," he garbled out. "No one has a key to *that* one."

"No. I'm not staying here. Give me my money. I didn't have to pay it all at once and I need it back."

It was a standoff. Neither of us said anything for some time.

"I can't do it," he said finally.

I knew, from the almost steady, slightly hunted expression on his face, that it was true. The money had been spent already. It was more than sun that was animating those bodies.

I had a sudden overview of my money's adventures, like that sort of map that shows with red lines where people have ventured. Beginning its life as a study-and-travel award bestowed upon the writer of a pretentious B.A. essay titled "The Caw of the Wild: Ted Hughes' Crow Poems," it trails across the Atlantic, losing substance like a comet, and tours the British Isles (missing Wales and Ireland for lack of time), and ends up, what's left of it, in some dark corner of West Hampstead where I can no longer follow its progress. Off the map.

"I'm going anyway," I said, hoisting my pack onto my shoulder.

"Well, I think you're stupid," he hissed with unusual energy, his morning spoiled, a little.

At this moment, the woman who had shown me to my room the day before appeared in the doorway, jigging with agitation.

"You're not leaving us dear?" she cried in alarm, and flew over to me with skinny hands waving. The ex-Scottish baker looked away.

To my dismay I found myself softening absurdly in the flurry of the woman's pathetic distress. My voice quavered as I spoke, and tears of exhaustion were uncomfortably near.

"Some people tried to get into my room last night. They had a key."

"Oh, don't go love, don't go. We'll give you another room to yourself. We'll put you nicely in Number Five down near us, won't we Pike? That's the one no one has a key for. Don't go love!"

"No, I can't stand it here," I replied, shaping each word deliberately. The woman's face collapsed into a geology of despair. She was helpless, but she stood in front of me and wouldn't move.

I did something then, something baroque and ugly. I shoved her. Her small body was in my way and then it was out of my way.

Pike didn't move. "Suit yourself," he said bitterly, and looked away from both of us. "Stupid," he mumbled again to himself, as I walked out into the bright day.

I spent my last three days in England in the most elegant flat I had seen in all my travels. It was part of a graceful Victorian house in a lovely part of London I had not known previously. The house was owned and fastidiously tended by a frail, fussy woman named Mrs. Peters. Mrs. Peters was the friend of parents of one of the students I had been in residence with while staying at the University. I called Patricia in desperation, remembering that she had said she would be staying in London during this period. We discovered that we were due to return to North America the same day, she to the U.S. and I to Canada. We spent our last few days weaving together another England story that involved a lot of café au lait, rapid anxious talk about home and men, and ignoring Mrs. Peters. Mrs. Peters was in quiet fits because her kitchen was being remodelled and I, a visitor, had seen it. (The exposed wires. The ragged plaster.)

But that first night, after Patricia and Mrs. Peters cooed sympathetically over my bad hostel experience, and then led me into that elegant Wedgwood-and-Persian rugs apartment (conveniently vacated by its Europe-hopping tenant), I went to bed early. I wanted to be alone. Lying in the clean dry sheets, feeling the soft blue coverlet around my shoulders, I slowly began to unclench. I hardly dared believe in the freedom my toes were exploring in this big, safe sleeping place.

That night, I dreamed of nothing.

How I Came to Serve a Moldy Piece of Pita Bread to k.d. lang's Roadie

It was because of not paying attention. I was distracted by a waiter kissing, on a whim, my bare summer shoulders, and I didn't look at the plate coming out from the kitchen. The roadie was very polite. k.d. did not tip me well. It was worse than no tip, and I don't blame her. In person, k.d. is as beautiful as her voice. She has translucent skin, and her eyes look like "Black Coffee" sounds.

When I was living in Toronto, in the eighties, I knew a man whose name I can't remember, because I called him Eeyore. He managed the bookstore where I worked sometimes when I wasn't waitressing at the Renaissance Café. He was mid-thirties, and he had a delicate, eruptive complexion and soft hair that flopped. He handled books very gently, with long white fingers, and he was kind to his staff. Once a woman came in from the large, ritzy hotel across the street and purchased nine hundred dollars worth of books. Eeyore stacked them up gingerly on the counter and asked the woman if she would be needing a milk crate.

Eeyore was sad. He did not have a woman to love and to fuck. This is what Eeyore wanted, in Toronto, in North America, in the 1980s. Once Paulina Poriskova, the model, came in the bookstore. Eeyore fell in love with her. After that, he always put the magazines with her covers in the front of the rack.

He was teaching me to process credit cards at the till. I was scared by the credit cards, by their flimsy plastic power. Eeyore was very patient with me, showing me how to slide the device over the credit card and paper slip, then what to fill in and what not to fill in. While he did this, he told me about his apartment.

"It's small," he said, "and very messy." He deftly removed a credit card slip from the tray. "Sometimes I don't feed myself for three days, and then I order a pizza. I eat pizzas and leave the crusts all over the place." He snorted softly, looking at me. "Once I was disturbed in my sleep by a pizza crust."

I was amused. I was twenty-four.

"Eeyore," I said, "what are you reading these days, in your little cramped, messy, pizza-filled apartment?"

"Molière. Rousseau's *Confessions*. I did my first degree in French, you know. I also have an M.L.S.—that's Library Science. Then no one would give me a job. I failed to get a job. I don't know how to put myself forward. I falter. *Je defaille.*"

"*Pourquoi est-ce que tu defaille?*" I said. I was wearing a charming black dress with an antique necklace of heavy pewter beads. I enjoyed the weight of the beads on my bare neck. I was newly married.

"*Parce-que je n'ai pas d'amour,*" Eeyore said, his eyes bright, excited, as if he'd just come in from hounds-and-hares.

Once in the bookstore, I caught out Lisa in a lie. Lisa was the owner of the shop. She was showing a wealthy local couple, an institution, around the store, and they asked her for a recommendation. Her hand darted out to a nearby display. It grasped Michael Ondaatje's new book.

"This is a *wonderful* book. It's about Toronto!" Her voice was a cross between razor blades and peach silk garters. Lisa had mentioned to me the night before that she had not read the book. She wouldn't remember saying a thing like that because she took too many pills.

The couple murmured interest. Lisa continued recklessly. "It's *quite* wonderful. All about the building of the big viaduct. Such graceful prose, just like swinging from girder to girder of the viaduct itself!"

Back cover, I thought.

The couple murmured again. The man inquired politely, in a crisp Eastern European accent, "Is it quite metafictional then? Is Ondaatje full-blown metafiction in this one?"

Lisa was stunned. I watched quietly, savagely, from the till, which was just far enough away that I could not be required to assist.

Out of nowhere, glided Eeyore.

"It is quite self-conscious," he said to the couple, "but there's still a good story there. He's definitely writing about writing—Ondaatje likes to pirouette, and often. But he pulls it off. And it *is* about Toronto."

The couple cooed, Lisa breathed, Eeyore took the book in his delicate digits, and I rang up the sale, credit.

I liked the bookstore, and I thought I liked Toronto, but my young husband and I had decided to go back to school and we had to move. We chose a school on the west coast, because of a friend's close-up photograph of a beach pea. A week before I was about to leave, Eeyore gave me a drawing. It was a perfectly realized Eeyore (not a tracing), standing in a field of grass that was represented by three or four blades. The donkey's head was slightly raised from its despondent droop. The simple caption read, "You Have Cheered Me Up." I put the drawing on my fridge with a magnet.

It was a busy night in the bookstore, the hot

August wind sweeping people in small frequent gusts from the Yorkville streets, little harvests of silk scarves and Armani trousers. Eeyore and I were working together on the two front tills. I was tired from packing boxes at home all day before my shift, and I was preoccupied with mental arrangements and rearrangements of my stuff and my life. At one point I forgot to check the expiry date on a credit card. Looking up from his own transaction, Eeyore swooped his hand into my tray to pick up the card. He showed me the mistake and politely explained to the ruffled customer that it was his card, not his person, that was unacceptable to us.

When the customers had thinned and we were idle, Eeyore asked if I'd be needing any more boxes for packing. He had piled some in the back for me. This was my last night at work, and I was leaving for the west in two days. He also thought I might be needing some good strong tape. He reached under the counter and produced a roll of packing tape, complete with dispenser and cutter. He held it out to me.

"Do you have time to meet for coffee before you go?" asked Eeyore.

I reached for the tape, which was perfect.

"We could meet at Chivas, tomorrow at six," he suggested, letting go of the tape.

"Fine," I said, grasping it.

I was busy. My husband and I were in a frenzy of box-packing, whirling around the apartment to Chopin's waltzes, then strutting to Ted Nugent's "Cat Scratch Fever," then, when we really needed a push, slide-bopping to Peter Gabriel's "Sledgehammer." We stopped for dinner, a pizza. We were happy, excited, about going on the road a long way. I had dreamed of Vancouver Island a few times now, seen it from above, like a map, an eerie glowing shelf gripped in the terrible energy of green things.

We resumed packing, while we made up a story of a woman who mated with a cougar and produced beautiful cougar-humans who stalked Bay Street. They would get into middle-management positions and then make wild, chaotic mergers with one another. Sometimes, in board meetings, they would say "meow" when they meant "now." Who would be the woman, we wondered. What would she look like?

"Like Paulina Poriskova," my husband suggested.

Game over. My stomach dropped. It was way past six, at least eight.

It is wonderful out here, the way the ocean gets in your eyes, and the wind on the beach blows everything out of your head. I am happy. These are the facts: I forgot to meet Eeyore for coffee and I forgot to look at the roadie's sandwich. I remember Eeyore's kind hands and the tilted dark beauty of k.d.'s eyes.

Dinner with the Devil

It was the third or so time I'd had dinner with the Devil. It's always hard to say for sure, because that's what the Devil is like.

This time it was Don, Don Avison. (Before, it was Ed. Before that, Shirley.) Don owned the small apartment building where we worked as his superintendents, cleaning and getting in new people when tenants gave notice. We were students, and the rent reduction for our services was a big deal. I was growing more and more pregnant and I enjoyed swinging pails of soapy water around my girth as I moved from stair to stair. I liked to work and sweat and feel my strength feeding the baby inside. I liked to go to tenants' apartments when they had trouble, and look at how they had their furniture and what books were on the shelves. One tenant had eighteen rows of adventure tales about American ex-military men. *Action Saigon, Live and Make Die, Bastard Brigade.* I added my own. *All Fucked Up and No Place to Go. Hate Party.*

Don, too, was a lover of all things American. But his taste ran to the more sophisticated, as we discovered when we were invited to dinner in appreciation for our services, me a week overdue. Peggy Lee crooned "Fever" from the stereo; on the album cover leaning on the console, Peggy herself popped out of a pink silk number that offered her breasts to us, creamy fruit from the fifties. Don's wife Angie, herself an aging fifties beauty, told us that they had recently gone down to the States to see Harry Connick Jr. in concert. When they put Harry on the stereo next, Chester and I had to admit that he was damn good.

We were going to have teriyaki steaks for supper, and Don was cooking. Chester got corralled into doing the man-talk-by-the-barbecue thing, and I went into the kitchen with Angie, who was making the salad. She was wearing some dull, expensive knit thing, but her cheekbones and ash-blonde bun fascinated me. She was tall and had, as they say, her figure.

"It'll change your life," she said, looking at my belly. "I had three." She smiled, not exactly warmly, but I assumed it was coming. "Labour's quite the experience."

I settled into my seat and chopped garlic contentedly.

"I was strapped down," Angie said, slicing spring onions, "hand and foot." She threw out her hands and feet with an energy that surprised me. The drama interfered with her slicing, so she put down the knife and the onions. "I screamed and screamed, the pain was so bad. I wanted to die." She resumed chopping. "And then Don came in. I looked right at him and I said 'I hate you'." The ash-blonde bun spun around as Don called from the patio for ice and fresh drinks. Angie had the drinks ready so fast that it seemed to me there had been a wrinkle in time, a tiny tuck, really, between the hate and the tray of balanced ice-cool drinks, wedges of lime. I thought of bones and crunching. Just before she glided out the patio door to serve the drinks to Don and Chester, Angie looked straight at me. "But it's *real*, you know. Real life."

Before dinner, Don showed us around the house. Thick beige carpets, immaculate Eaton's furniture, expensive and unexceptional, except for one thing, a carving, from Africa Don said, brought back by an American friend on a buying trip. It was a man, carved from dark glossy wood. The man's body was elongated as he stretched his neck up and pursed his full lips into a howl or song. Don explained that it was the last in a series of carvings done by an artist who was greatly revered in the village where he lived. When the artist died, Don's friend bought up all the available carvings. Don liked this one, so his friend gave it to him.

"No doubt," said Don, "those nigs can carve. That and their big black dongs."

Chester had remarked to me once that Don was one of those very *clean* sort of alcoholics. It was true—he always wore immaculate pressed clothes. The first thing he showed us when we took the job was a baseball bat that he kept in the storage room. It was there because a business partner had done a dirty. If Don found the partner, there would be the bat.

At one point Don confiscated a collection of religious tapes that belonged to a black man who had been having revival meetings in one of the business suit below the apartment. We used our keys to get into the storage room and get the tapes. We listened to them and then gave them back to the man. Don wasn't angry, because we were only naive and had a lot to learn about nigs. Also about pakis, who curried rats and didn't use toilet paper. We would come into our whiteness, come to inhabit it like a natty pale suit.

The steaks were very, very, very tender. They had soaked all day in the sauce and gave pure pleasure in the mouth. They were served with steamed asparagus in béchamel sauce. I decided to drink some red wine because I hadn't had any in nine months and one week and I figured that I had waited long enough, the ball was in the baby's court now. We all drank wine and had seconds of everything. Harry Connick Jr. sang "It had to be You," sweeter than Sinatra. Don's youngest daughter Maureen came through the front door halfway through the meal and joined us. We did "Saturday Night Live" skits. Don was intelligent and funny in his appreciation and recreation of the penis routine. I laughed and Chester laughed, really laughed. Don's daughter laughed. Don told Angie to get more wine, and she was up from the table. Her lips stretched back over her teeth.

"Don and Maureen get along so well now. Not like when Maureen was a kid and she was scared shitless of him." Angie glided into the kitchen and at once reappeared with wine. "Shitless," she repeated, and set the bottle in front of Don, with a thump.

"If you don't want to drive home later," Don said to Chester, nodding at the wine, "you two can stay here tonight."

"It'll be O.K.," said Chester, "I haven't really had that much." He hadn't. I hadn't either. But I knew that we both felt very, very drunk. We had dipped our toes in the river of blackness that roared underneath the table, the carpet, the house, the world.

"But you might want to sleep with Maureen," Don continued. "Your wife's too far gone to be any good to you right now."

"I got my figure back after each one, even Maureen," said Angie. Maureen was twenty-two. I thought that she was uglier than her mother, with coarser features and less drama. She was a quiet editor for a wedding magazine.

We finished our meal. I was surprised and slightly annoyed that there was no dessert. I had a craving for a dessert. I really wished for a light cheesecake with fruit, or some fat strawberries enrobed in chocolate. Such a something should have followed the exquisite dinner. I had a small anger at this deprivation.

After dinner we sat in the Eaton's furniture in the living room and chatted, but the party had already peaked. Angie perched on her chair, seeming not to make a dent in it. In a while we were moving towards the door.

"Oh, wait a minute!" said Don, "there's one room I forgot to show you!" He herded us down the hallway and in through a door. The room was quite empty except for a large bed. There was a bear skin spread on it. The legs of the bear, or where they would have been, hung over the four corners of the bed almost touching the floor, a polished blonde wood.

"The bedroom," announced Don. We were quiet. "We don't use it much anymore."

Chester and I moved back to the foyer where Angie was waiting. Don came up behind. There were exit shufflings, thank yous, gettings-on of heavy fall coats. And I swear, somewhere in there, was something else. It was a papery, dry slip of a whisper. It was said by Don, and Angie's bones rustled it beneath her clothes. It was:

"Stay and suck and fuck with us."

I never *heard* it said, in the foyer, but I knew later it had been said. That's how it is with the Devil. You never hear it and you never see it and time is wrinkled and oh boy things are odd. But you knew all along.

As we drove home from dinner in the dark Chester and I looked only once at each other, frightened in the black pools of our everywhere eyes.

One night when our baby boy was a few months old, Chester and I were up late watching Johnny Carson. We were dead tired, but we needed to grab a few banal Carson moments for ourselves. A slick aging actress was thrashing around the hard lines of her body, telling an anecdote. She hissed the word "tits" once to show she could use it. Johnny did his naughty-mommy grimace. Chester and I, slumped against each other on the couch, rode up and down on the machine-gun rounds of laughter.

Suddenly we were paying attention. Harry Connick Jr. had come out from behind the curtain and was being applauded. He sat beside the actress and greeted her. There was something about his walking and sitting and greeting that made the audience quiet. The jigging, greedy laughter stopped. Johnny asked Harry some questions about his background and music, and Harry answered them. He didn't put down Johnny and he didn't put down himself. He quietly answered the questions as if they had been asked of him. The interview was over.

Harry is young, white, male, handsome, and wealthy. He has gleaming dark hair and bright, straight teeth. But there is something about him. That he smiles when he says the words "my family." That he dips his head to consider. That he just seems like somebody's beautiful son.

How to detail grace?

But Johnny and Chester and I and millions of North Americans—and maybe Don and Angie— watched it move across a stage, slip around a curtain, and disappear.

Sweet Blood

The young man and woman and their baby son found a place to camp, and set up their tent and equipment about thirty yards from the clean cold water of Lake Superior. They were high on the first leg of their journey across the country and on the craggy northern shore they'd discovered and on the way the baby's round head and fat cheeks looked against the lake-soaked blue of the sky. The campsite was only seven dollars, and in the bargain, they got a proprietress who was odd, a manless mother of nine who left an impression of blowsy gingham and log-whacking as she bustled about her place giving asthmatic orders to her handyman brother-in-law. Her children populated different parts of the campground. One of them, who worked in the camp store, was a fifteen-year-old girl whose adolescence was popping out of her jeans. She managed to be rather friendly to the young couple, recommending a certain brand of bug spray for the baby, even though she laboured under a treacherously balanced coif as sweet and tangled as a bee could want. Her eyes peered out of raccoon make-up at the baby, and she smiled and said he was real cute. Another of the woman's children, a small boy, attached himself to the young couple.

At first they hardly noticed him. But when they did notice him, mid-afternoon, they realized he had been hanging around all day, hovering here and there with the jittery ephemerality of a fruit fly. They began to speak to him and ask him all sorts of questions about the campsite and the area: where was the wood, where could they swim, what was the name of the current that disturbed the glassy inlet they were perched on? He knew a lot and the couple exchanged amused glances. How old was he? He was twelve. A current of mild surprise rippled through the couple. He was very small for his age.

Small for his age, but yes, they could see that he had to be something like twelve considering his ugly, ferret-wise features. He looked like a shrunken-apple doll, with his tiny face, largish flattish nose, and protruding but skinny lips. His gerbil-coloured hair stuck out all ways, and he wore a plaid shirt in which the light sections might once have been grey, but no longer were. His intense but unfocussed stare darted to the woman now and again, and avoided the man. When the man straightened his pants after bending to put in a tent peg, though, the boy gave his own pants an exaggerated hitch. He was quiet at first, but once he started talking he kept up a running commentary on things as he sat at the picnic table with the couple, or strode manfully, his little wide pant legs going flap flap, as he wandered around the grounds. The couple were very amused with their find. The best part was that his name was Vern, and Vern was twelve.

"That's Montreal River goin' out to the lake there. And around that point of land, see, there, that's the tourist beach, it's sandy, it's good swimming. It sure takes a lot of responsibility to be a father, it sure does, that's why it's good to be a man to have a baby, to be able to handle it. That baby might be one of them fat kids when it gets bigger."

"Yes, it takes a *lot* of responsibility to have a baby," she said, "you have to change them, feed them, carry them when they cry, make sure they don't hurt themselves . . ." The woman was enjoying herself immensely.

"Is that why you waited so long?" he said. "Lots of responsibility. Baby Homer cries all night long and my sister never sleeps. Baby Ig died, stopped breathing, my sister Ezzie got a plastic thing."

Baby Homer. Baby Ig. Esmerelda. Soon the woman had the whole motley, baby-worn crew of Vern's sisters and their infants named forth into the sunny blue day, Vern cooperating with all questions, lining up names and ages as efficiently as he named water depths and wood types. Then he sped off on his bike to answer his mother's yell.

When he came back, he was quieter, poking around the graves of fires with a long stick. The couple were quieter too, looking forward to the night and the fire they would make. Still, Vern managed a brief summation of his concerns.

"I think about the future sometimes. I think about what kind of wife I'm going to have, what kind of truck, what kind of boat, what kind of job. Real important things." The couple giggled without a sound. Then Vern also noted that while the man's truck was O.K., Ford trucks were better.

The man wanted to go swimming on the rocky shore near their tent. Vern had said that it wasn't very good swimming there, but the man wanted to try anyway. He got his shorts on in the tent while Vern and the woman and the baby settled themselves in chairs on the rocky shore. The woman held the baby on her knee and stroked the delicious smooth hillocks of his shoulders, bending over occasionally to kiss his hair, the tiny lobes of his ears, his blue-veined temples. Vern and she watched the man wade into the water up to his ankles. He called back that the rocks were very slippery and then continued to stand, gazing out at the lake.

Looking up momentarily from the baby's sweet humid skin, the woman noticed that Vern was watching her. "I decided," he said, "I like it when girls wear a little bit of make-up. I don't like it when they wear a lot of make-up and I don't like it when they wear no make-up, I like when they wear just a little stuff around here." He had an odd way of saying his "s," so that "stuff" came out "shtuff." The woman laughed prettily and tossed her head back to the sun a little more energetically than was necessary to get the hair out of her subtly rimmed eyes. Then she cuddled the baby into herself.

The man was shouting back that it really was very slippery. He wanted his swim, but it really was very slippery. He remained ankle-deep, undecided. The woman, relieved that it looked as if the man was not going to be swimming near the river current she had worried about, encouraged her husband to come out. "We're not expecting a show," she said laughing. He smiled and turned towards them, balancing himself on the slippery rocks.

"I am." Vern was sitting calmly in his chair with his skinny arms folded, but the pitch of his voice had altered slightly, buzzing with some faint excitement. "I am. I want a show all right!" The man still smiled, hard, as he came out of the water.

The man and the woman were getting things out of the cooler for supper. It looked as if Vern was joining them to eat. The man told him that he'd better go ask his mother if it was all right if Vern ate with them, as he wouldn't want to be responsible for spoiling anyone's dinner plans. When ten minutes had passed without Vern's return, the man announced to the woman that the mother had probably wanted Vern to stay in his own house. Just then Vern's bicycle, with Vern astride, appeared on the path leading to the campsite.

"She don't care if I stay, so I will," he said.

The woman had gone the long path to the outhouse and got talking on the way back to Vern's uncle, who had accidentally cut off his hand with a chainsaw in Timmins. When she got back to the campsite Vern was industriously hunched over the picnic table, putting together the cheap hibachi they had just bought in Sault St. Marie. Vern didn't look up as she approached, but made a grunting gesture towards her husband, and addressed her. "He wanted me to do this because he has no goddamn idea how to put these things together. I've done lots of 'em." The husband murmured to his wife that this did not describe the situation quite precisely, and the woman's delighted laugh floated up and then came down, like a soft sheet, over the heads of her husband beside her, Vern at the table, and the baby in his playpen.

Vern lit into his hot dogs like a starved cat, but found time between bites to comment on this and that. Baby Homer loved hot dogs and nearly choked on one once. Vern's own bedtime was ten o'clock, but he sometimes stayed awake in his bed thinking until twelve or later. Did the baby want some hot dogs? Oh, thinking about important things, his future and so on. Evinrude was the best boat, but SeaBlade was O.K., that was the kind his uncle had. His aunt from Timmins was coming later that night so he might get another meal! He wished that there was more than just blueberries for dessert. He liked donuts and flipjackets. No, not flapjacks, flipjackets. He ate them at his sister's. Etta didn't have a husband anymore because he went to live with Sue-Lynn. Sue-Lynn was O.K. She had three babies. It was a good thing he had got the damn hibachi together or they wouldn't have been able to eat at all. Was the man going to go for his swim yet?

Purple dusk, which had stolen upon them as they ate, brought out the bugs. The woman was being eaten alive. She said that aloud, "They're eating me alive, they always do," and remembered for some reason what her mother said when she'd told her that she was still breast-feeding every two hours. "He's eating you alive she'd said," her tone proud, horrified. The bugs really were out in full force now, and the woman couldn't help complaining because it looked as if her husband and Vern weren't too bothered.

"It's because girls got sweet blood," Vern said. "The bugs like the sweetness, that's what my mom says. He gestured at the man. "*We* don't got sweet blood."

"The bugs *are* girls," said the man. "Only the female mosquitoes bite."

The woman couldn't stand the bugs any longer, and abandoned her blueberries to fetch wood for a fire. She intended to saturate herself with wood smoke, which the bugs didn't like. Sleep would be impossible unless she could get away from these mosquitoes. She started up the path to the camp store where the firewood was piled; soon she was running and slapping her legs. When she got inside the store she was still slapping and shooing, and the woman there invited her to sit down for a few minutes while she searched the back room for some bug lotion that the northerners knew really worked, if you could stand the odour.

When the woman got back to the campsite, wheelbarrow full of wood, and smelling like turpentine, it was darker. Vern and her husband, still eating, sat opposite each other at the table. When she got closer she could see that her husband had scrounged some old donuts they had forgotten about from the junk in the back seat of the truck, and that the two of them were munching silently.

They didn't look up. Each was looking at his dough-nut and reaching for another. She began building her fire a little ways off from the picnic table, en-joying the quiet, and the glassy lake, now amethyst. Lake Superior was really very superior, she thought, enjoying her bad joke as well. And soon I'll have double insurance against these mosquitoes.

Quite suddenly, the calm was ripped by a sharp voice coming from the larger of the two figures hunched at the picnic table.

"You've already had more than your share, you little pig, that was my doughnut," the voice said. It could have been a joke but all the lightness had gone out of it. The man himself was surprised by his voice in the dark dusk, naked and sharp.

Vern continued to sit quietly, then the man tried to joke with him about his piggishness. Vern chewed what was left in his mouth slowly and carefully, as if aware that this was the only way he could be prop-erly rid of it. Then all at once he jumped on his bike, said "thanks for dinner" to the ground under the picnic table, and disappeared into the night. After he had gone the couple tried briefly to enjoy the queerness of the boy, joking thinly about how he would be back for breakfast. Then they put the baby to bed in the tent and started their fire and talked about the important things in their future.

The couple and the baby woke up early the next morning, so early that it was before check-out time on the grounds. The place was silent except for the birds, everybody shrouded in tents, trailers or cabins, dopey with sleep. They decided to go anyway; the morning was perfect, and they were excited about crossing the Ontario-Manitoba border. They packed quickly, left the wheel-barrow beside the dead fire-ring, and got the baby strapped into his car seat. As they pulled out, past the store and woodpile, down the long gravel road to the highway, the woman had a strange sneaky feeling as she made her getaway.

Just after they passed the "Welcome to Manitoba" sign, the woman remembered something from when she was a teenager. She looked out the window of the truck and remembered an ice rink she used to go to with her friends. They used to mill around in the snack area and in the hallways behind the male change room and sometimes even pretend to watch the hockey games, but it was all about being near certain sweaty boys. One of these boys, who was not her favourite, would talk with her whenever he could. He was ugly in a startling, nearly attractive way, but when she talked about him to her friends she just said he was ugly. And stupid. There was a dirty white cat that would sometimes hang around the arena too, and this ugly boy would sometimes bring the cat to her and stroke it. She would stroke it too, because she liked cats. She also, one time, as he was stroking and she was stroking the cat, let her fingers touch his fingers, all in the motion of stroking. Something exploded under her ribs. He called her the next day to ask her to go out with him. When she heard his voice on the phone she knew the faint thrill of the electrician when he pulls the switch he's been wiring. It works. And then she finished the job cleanly, telling him that she had to take care of her sick grandmother indefinitely, hanging up the phone quickly just in time. And then called her friends and said, Ew, ew, Jamie Cribs, how gross. The woman didn't know why she was remembering all this, barrelling into Manitoba and scratching her mosquito bites.

Snackers

"Hey!" I ran over the weedy yard, up the steps and onto the porch where Chester was sitting with *Being and Nothingness*. "Vern's burning again. Piles of it. He just put a nightgown on the fire and what looks like about a hundred kewpie dolls. Mary's peeved!"

Chester and I moved to where we could see and not be seen. Vern was still there, across the street, heaping garbage onto the homemade incinerator in his front yard. His wife Mary, a sheep-perm atop a loose flowered cotton shift, poked her head around the side of the house and called his name again. Vern continued to pile things on the fire—shoes, metal scraps, picture frames, bunches of dried seaweed, bits of cloth, egg shells—and he clamped his features into a stubborn, cretinous smirk.

"Listen to me!" Mary thundered, her enormous breasts shifting around in her dress like agitated bowling balls. "*Listen!*" Vern's whey-faced smirk deepened into a scowl. He didn't reply to his wife. Steadily, he forked onto the blaze newspapers, flyers, ancient magazines. I swear I saw the young Joan Crawford, heavy-browed, carmine-mouthed, licked up into the flames. Vern poked the fire with satisfaction, stoked and poked, and ignored for the fourth time Mary's call.

"VERN! Come here now! Now! NOW! The bowling breasts were wild, independent, frenzied. Vern did not come to them. Abruptly, Mary turned and entered the back door to the house.

Chester and I were weak-kneed, helpless. We snorted, we giggled, we collapsed. When our laughter wore itself out, we went to the house to make love before our baby woke up from his nap.

We expected to say a neighbourly hello now and then, on our quiet, scrubby Victoria street, to Vern and Mary and their elusive, skulking live-in son Harold. We knew we would see Vern occasionally cutting the grass and burning things in burning season; we would see Mary pop in and out of the house, German cottage-clock style. We expected to watch their spectacular tawdry fights from the porch of our spectacular tawdry rented house. Such lovely semi-squalor that year: their squabbles; our scratched hard-wood floors; high ceilings with half-installed quarter-round; useless, enchanting nooks.

What we did not expect was to be invited for Christmas drinks.

Vern took my sweater at the door. "Are you sure I can't take off anything else for you?" He chuckled, winking at Chester in the tiny, darkly lit hallway. Mary bustled up from somewhere inside the house.

"You come right in, right in." Her eyes, magnified greatly by the thick lenses of her glasses, were anxious, maternal, peeled for any discomfort Vern with his antics might cause to guests in her home. She cooed at our little boy, who was frisking about at our heels on his new sea-legs. "What a sweet child! What a sweet little boy. You come right on in for some cookies. All of you come on in, right this way for some snackers."

As our eyes adjusted to the semi-dark, the crazy piles grew into focus. (My ebony elf—who always knows—knew there would be something.) I first thought of old widows, of a hundred plates of cat food, of chickens strung on a laundry wire, of rats and fruit rinds dark with flies.

But it was not quite decay here, not filth. It was, in every room we passed, deliberate, piled, ordered—years upon years of papers, doilies, boxes, small appliances (toasters, ancient Mix Masters, irons, lamps—shaded, unshaded, with plaster mermaids, without—can openers), folded clothing (folded pants, folded breast-feeding nightgowns, folded flower shifts with ruffles, shifts without), candle holders, ceramic lambs carrying baskets for a candle, ceramic lambs not carrying candle-baskets but signs saying "You're so cute," plastic place mats from Nevada. In some places it reached the ceiling, truly. One tiny room was pure in its exclusive devotion to hatboxes: large, small, laced, plain, beribboned, crushed. The place smelled faded but clean, and the hallway was clear. Somehow Vern had got Chester into a dim room along the hallway, and I was walking, Cal toddling, behind Mary. We were moving deeper into the house.

Suddenly I bridled. I returned along the hallway, letting Cal follow Mary, and peered into the tiny room where Vern had Chester in a man's man elbow grip. This room was less crowded than the others and featured a narrow bed, corners tucked in with naval precision, and a small T.V. set. "It's mine. Mary don't come in here," Vern was saying. "I hide out here when the nagging gets to me." Vern's face crinkled into a grin. "You know what I'm saying, eh? It goes on and on and. . . . Hey, I bet you like war photos. Take a gander at that picture." Vern led Chester close to the far wall where a black-and-white photograph featured rows of men, some standing, some hunkered, in a muddy field. "Pick out yours truly, go on!" Chester scanned for a moment, then pointed without energy to one of the time-blurred faces. "Hooey—no!" That's Clive Baker, he was an accountant before the war. He was—liked the *boys*, if you take my meaning, didn't like the ladies. That's not me in that picture, oh no, not a bit. Wrong-o! Try again."

Then they saw me. Something in Vern switched gears. He peered at me closely, face so still for a moment that it assumed a bizarre intelligence. "You have fair hair, it's fair isn't it. But when I was young I had really blonde hair, white blonde. I can prove it too." Still watching me, alert to pending protests of disbelief, he reached for a rusty vial on his small dresser. Unscrewing the lid, he pulled out a small tangle of milkweed. "My baby hair," he pronounced. "My sister cut it off when I was a baby." We looked at the hair. It was very blonde, indeed.

"Snackers!" Mary boomed from somewhere. We were still looking at the hair glowing faintly in the dim room, and could not move. Then Mary was at the doorway. The huge mothering insect stare rested on me, then Chester, and then aimed at Vern. "Are you keeping these folks from their refreshments? Are you holding them up with your high jinks? Come on now. To the living room. You must be starved, dear!" she said, tapping me on the flat stomach I was so proud of after Cal.

We trooped down the hallway and were led into the living room. More piles reigned, but there were also free couches—about seven or eight, arranged at impossible angles to each other as if recently abandoned by a convention of schizophrenic elves. We all sat in the couches (still warm from elfin hindquarters) except Cal, who busied himself in the bog of junk on the floor. We had a couch each, and twisted ourselves into awkward positions so that we could see each other.

Almost as soon as we had sat down, Mary whisked herself into the adjoining room, and returned, several times, with trays and bottles of beer. She placed a paper lace doily under each beer. Vern said to Cal, "Cutie boy! Look at Uncle Vernie," and pulled his face into an unearthly goofiness. Cal looked briefly and, colossally unimpressed, returned to his treasures. Finally Mary stopped whisking and settled her bulk into a sofa. The beer was good and cold, just like beer in any living room. Vern said they were from Saskatchewan. We said we'd moved out from Ontario. The social engines were beginning to rev with a small but steady hum. Hamilton, blah, blah, Saskatoon, blah, blah, snow, blah, flowers, blah, hum, hum, yes really, hum.

After about half a beer, suddenly ravenous, I approached the cakes and pastries and devoured several greedily. They were shockingly sweet, but I gorged a steady stream, cooing to Mary about delicious, delicious.

"They make me fart," contributed Vern, swallowing a rum ball whole, and Mary glared. Vern winked at Chester, licked his index finger, and held it up to punctuate the strike.

"Thinks he's Sonny and Cher," she said. Cal toddled to the table, took into his mouth what looked like a wedge of icing, and grimaced. He simply opened, and, little god that he was, let the globs of sugared saliva drop without ceremony onto the coffee table. Then, becoming theatrical under our watching, he spit the remaining bits out with a wry glance and much exaggerated puffing until he was bored and returned to his junk pile. Vern was in stitches and Mary relaxed under the influence of this universal and heartwarming spectacle.

"The fruit cake is really nice," I said, riding the momentum.

"Yeah, great," Chester added.

There was sudden quiet.

"You really like that fruitcake?" Mary peered at me, looking for signs of treachery.

"Yes, yes, I really like it. It's moist, *very* moist!" I was insistent, convincing, barely shrill.

And then Mary singled me out, latched me. Her eyes deepened, softened, and we were at a wedding, a funeral, a swearing-in. Glance still locked with mine, she hoisted herself, her breasts jiggling gently, and said "Come into the pantry."

The pantry was intensely cluttered but clean. Mary, still solemn, reached up into a cupboard and withdrew a biscuit tin, which she placed onto the counter. After unsealing the lid with a deft finger, she lifted, reverently, an aromatic cheese-clothed bundle. We were still. She looked at me again, not speaking. I tried.

"So, this is how you make them? With cheese-cloth?"

Clearly, this was not it. But I guessed, from Mary's still-connected gaze, that what I'd said was simply irrelevant, not disastrous. I tried again.

"You age them for a good while? In the tin?"

Now Mary was impatient. One breast twitched slightly. She lowered the bundle into one of a number of empty coffee tins on the counter, and sealed the lid with a snap. She looked at me again, pleadingly, giving me one more chance. I relented.

"For me?"

That was it. The buggish orbs filled with love.

"Yes dear," she whispered, "Yes." And gently took me back to the living room.

Vern and Chester were discussing the origins of the couches. Garage sales, ancient furniture ware-house blow-outs. Mary resettled herself and had something to say.

"Well, there's the couches that are here. And the

couches that aren't." She looked at Vern and they clicked. There was an Ingmar Bergman silence while a clock ticked. There was breathing. I ate another rum ball. Vern whistled through his teeth, a long, low blizzard on a night train through Saskatchewan.

"By all rights you should be setting there in a real leather sofa," said Mary. "Real soft leather too. Beautiful colour, 'Calf Sunset' they called it in the catalogue."

"Yep. It was—excuse me, *is*, they still *have* it—a beaut of a couch," Vern said. Vern nodded at Mary in complete agreement. Mary bobbed her head back. And—bob, bob, bob, bob—they repeated the ritual of their furious intimacy.

"Leather couch?" Chester inquired politely.

Vern cocked his head, smirked, and made us wait. As if we could have figured it out easily enough. "Cousin Nick and Sheila kept it after Gram Kester died. They were supposed to be *storing* it for us—"

"Hmph, *storing*—" Mary grunted with satisfaction.

"*Storing* it. But they *kept* it. It's still in Saskatoon, fifteen years now. Quite something, eh?" In perfect unison, Vern and Mary sat in two not-leather couches. We sipped our beer. I steered Cal away from some glass trinkets on a low table. Chester took a rum ball.

"That's really sad," I said, "about your couch. Some people can be very—very insensitive."

I was really off. Worse than before, in the kitchen. Mary skewered me again with the bug-eye beam.

"But things don't really matter, do they honey? A couch is just a couch, I always say. They can keep their old couch, for all I care. It's *people* that matter, not any old couches. I say it's *people* that matter. Don't you feel that way? People matter, things don't, right?"

Chester wasn't expected to say anything, and didn't. It was me she'd targeted. I was the one who'd grow bowling balls, raise fruitcakes, place doilies.

I was saved by the shadowy appearance, in the fake-bricked archway to the livingroom, of Harold.

"Company?" he said in a subdued but genial voice. Then he stoop-glided softly to an empty sofa and settled himself gingerly into it. He was thirtyish, pale, and slightly humpbacked. What I had taken for a skulk, from across the street, was probably only some minor brain damage.

"Harold!" exclaimed Vern. "This is our son, Harold. These folks come over for a little Christmas cheer, Harold. Chester, can you believe it took us seventeen years to get him? Seventeen years!" Vern looked at me and tried for a leer, then glanced over at Cal, who had busied himself in a new pile of flea-market gold. "Didn't take you two long. Not long at all! Mary was getting on a bit when Harold finally come along. I just don't know what took so long. Not much of a medical man."

"But he did come along," remarked Mary.

"I really hope you're comfortable," Harold said, looking at each of Chester and me in turn.

"Oh, yes," I said.

"Yes," said Chester.

"Seventeen years!" whistled Vern, chuffing through that Saskabush night. "Why could it take so long? You should look in one of them books you always got your nose in, Mary!"

"More fruit cake? Another beer?" inquired Mary. Breasts jostled, shifting, itching to serve.

"No, thanks," I said.

"Thanks, no," said Chester.

"Are your stomachs too full?" asked Harold with concern. "I certainly hope you're not too full! An overly full stomach can be very uncomfortable."

"Maybe we were doing it wrong!" Vern's face doubled on itself in mirth, like an imploding monkey's. Mary glared with mechanical irritation. Harold asked us if we would like pillows, to make us more comfortable.

We were quiet on the way home, across the street and up the porch steps. But we rallied. It didn't take long. I put Cal to sleep and came into our bedroom where Chester was waiting. I straddled him and leaned close to his ear.

"Snackers," I said. "I want some snackers." We snorted, we giggled, we collapsed all over each other. I wriggled out of my underwear, and slipped my hand inside Chester's. We kissed, we were young. We had a little god of a boy, such a smart one, such a healthy one, we'd made him by accident, we didn't even try. "Let's fuck," one of us said. Oh, we weren't even thirty yet, our bodies were firm, our quarrels were dense, artistic. So we fucked and fucked. And fucked some more.

Just because I'd forgotten the fruitcake that was no reason not to, was it?

A Midsummer Night's Biker Party

"Your fantasies are dumb."

"Who are you to judge my fantasies?"

"They're repetitive, and they always end with you marshmallowing into some guy's arms, and then the screen goes fuzzy."

Bill was right. Moira's fantasies were dumb. Bill's were dumb, too. His always ended with him telling someone something, and good. They were two humans with dumb fantasies, walking around on this earth, which is spinning in a lot of black space.

One recent evening Bill and Moira went to a midsummer's party, at Alice's. It was something else. It didn't put a halt to all the dumbness and sadness and cruelty. But it was something else.

Alice was a woman who rode and liked motorcycles—a biker woman, Moira called her. Moira met Alice in the Primary Education Programme, where they had wanted to be teachers. Soon Alice didn't want to be a teacher any more. No one wanted her to have tattoos or draw witches with berets instead of pointed hats. No one, not the teachers she helped in schools or her classmates who wrote in big, round hands, wanted to see or know about her tattoos, her days on the streets. They didn't want her, she didn't want them, her husband said they were all pricks, she was away from home too much.

Alice liked Moira a little, partly because Moira didn't have the confidence to dislike anyone. Sometimes a person needs a bit of that. But maybe there was more to it, more than that dreary business. Alice saw something in Moira crouched there, waiting. Alice couldn't see it clearly and didn't, frankly, think much would come of it. Moira looked all mushy, drew squinchy eyes and apologetic lopsided smiles on her peer critiques because she couldn't say anything bad. But Alice noticed once in a while how Moira's eyes would focus on a distant object, sometimes a mountain, and hold it. Not exactly get yer engines running, get out on the highway, but something.

So Alice invited Moira and Bill, her long-time

whatever, to a summer goodbye party. Alice and Beefer were saying goodbye again, saying hello this time to somewhere in Alberta. Bill made jokes to Moira about biker bashes until a few days before the party, and then he went silent on the subject.

The house was full of biker things. Photos of bikes with good paint jobs standing alone, back wheels canted like hips. Photos of people on bikes: Alice, pregnant astride an old Indian; Beefer, before he was her husband, standing beside his first bike at seventeen. Bike posters; bike parts, nailed to the walls. Steppenwolf playing in the background.

The barbecue was out back, the talk already in first gear when Moira and Bill arrived. Alice was nice, gave them cans of beer, and introduced them all around the picnic table. Alice had good manners. She told Moira once that she got them from the Hell's Angels, where a person always knew what was expected.

There was a woman named Mikey there who had done a painting of Alice on a bike. It was a goodbye present. It was done in rich dark colours, and it put Alice in a noble pose, nose lifted to the wind, hands gripping handlebars with almost dainty grace. The eyes were strong and sad. Mikey was explaining that she had put it in the style of the Dutch Renaissance, which was all about making art out of the daily activities of ordinary people. Moira didn't know if this was true or not.

Moira was a little scared of Mikey, with her long legs and no make-up, with a child, a boy of six running around the yard. She didn't seem like a biker, although later it turned out that she did have a small bike, which she rode up a mountain every once in a while. At regular intervals, like her period, said Mikey loudly. Bill didn't hear that; he was talking to Mikey's husband, who made signs. The sign-maker was a good-natured man made of knotty muscles. Bill seemed to be enjoying himself.

Moira had another beer. There was talk of the motor pig. It seemed that one of Alice and Beefer's trucks needed to be taken away. For some reason it had to go to Vancouver to be landed in the yard of an asshole. It was a bad truck, and it needed to go to a bad person. During all this talk, Moira had the feeling of being edged off her seat, although no one was really near enough to do this. Everyone was nice to her. She focussed on each face. The motor pig probably wouldn't make it to the ferry but someone had to try, and the person to try was Reb, with his new wife Sue. (The old wife had left one of Reb's bikes to rot in an abandoned chicken yard. There was so much chicken shit, there were mushrooms growing in it.) Reb sat right there at the picnic table and grinned. He and Sue were going soon, after the hot dogs, to take the motor pig. At one point Reb said something that sounded to Moira like a poem:

Nothin' wrong with lookin' like Charles Manson

Nothin' wrong with thinkin' like Charles Manson
Somethin' wrong with actin' like Charles
Manson . . .

There were the hot dogs. Moira helped Alice hand them out. Moira thought: What is this? Do I like it? What is good? Reb, and Sue, with her dark fall of hair and coon-eyes, had to go right away. When the motor pig roared and grunted away behind the tall fence in the back yard and down the road to the ferry, Moira cheered with the rest. She was so excited she was scared. It reminded her of a dream she once had about being stuck, forever, at the edge of coming.

The Beatles came on the outdoor speakers, "Piggies." It was too much. Alice came out of the house, laughing. She had made it happen. Moira thought how she loved Alice's laugh. It ripped right out of her.

Jay laughed and showed very straight white teeth. Jay was very straight. He was Alice and Beefer's neighbour. He had an interest in prairie architecture and bikes. These interests prepared him for what he had undertaken: he was going to be part of a caravan going to Alberta, a caravan of Alice, Beefer, their son Beef Stew (Stew for short), and the possessions of Alice, Beefer, and Stew. Also Jay himself, who was unemployed, recently separated from his girlfriend, and curious. He would drive a truck, have an adventure, and drive back to the coast. His girl-friend didn't know how to be by herself, said Jay. She was nice; he wished her no ill will. He saw her last night when she came to pick up some stuff from his house, but he didn't have anything to tell her.

Jay kept some bees, and listened to big band music, a hangover from his childhood when his father wouldn't let them listen to anything else. Jay had shortish dark hair that was very glossy. What was it as glossy as, Moira wondered. It's as glossy as Beefer's is long. As mine is safely tucked under with a curling iron to take the edge off its straightness. Moira was a bit drunk, and a bit stoned now too. She was trying to imagine the inside of Jay's house, his books on prairie architecture, his coming over to Alice and Beefer's to talk about bikes. Did Jay touch the bikes in Beefer's workshop or only look? What did they say? Where was the father now with his Glen Miller records?

Beefer told a story about scaring some Jehovah's Witnesses with his penis through a mail slot. Jay embellished it, saying what if, what if, what if the Witnesses told their children it was part of God's plan. They'd have to tell them something, wouldn't they? Moira couldn't take her eyes off him. He wasn't nervous about his contribution. He was wearing his straight white shirt and dark pants. God's plan, only slightly funny, slipped into the mix.

Jay laughed and showed his straight white teeth.

Moira thought: Who are you? She put in her mind a list of all she knew.

1. Jay used to be an electrician.
2. Jay spent time with Alice and Beefer looking at? talking about? touching? bikes.
3. Jay was very polite to Moira, asking her if she found the College classes pleasant. He said *find*, do you *find* them pleasant. Maybe his father said that he *found* Glen Miller to be the best.
4. Jay was tall and thin, but not skinny.
5. He liked independent women, but wished well those who were not.
6. He was going to Alberta with Alice and Beef Stew and Beefer. With Beefer, who likes Mikey's paintings but doesn't like the idea of mixed bike clubs because the women get too fuckin' mouthy.
7. Jay was one of a number of humans in the seventeenth back yard of Alice and Beefer, one summer night.

More beers, a few tokes, some bikers, some not. Alice knew all kinds of people. That was the biker party.

Sitting in class on Monday morning, staring out at the mountains, Moira imagined the caravan trailing its way to Alberta. Beefer seemed to like Alice, and vice versa. Alice was probably laughing. Whatever else it was all about, little wedges of darkness or sickness, they liked each other. How often does that happen?

Then she was thinking about Jay. In her fantasy, which takes place in winter, he is not coming towards her, to envelop her in rapture. He is walking along the sea wall, looking at some distant ships with great interest. He sees her and smiles, his white teeth. His hair is shiny, his outline's crisp in the winter sun, and he is interested in his ships.

Moira, in her fantasy, is thinking about whether Alice is happy or sad. She is thinking about Alice, and Jay is thinking about his ships. They pass on the sea wall, nod to one another. Jay's beautiful hair, dark against the white sky. Jay, apart. All of them—Jay, Moira, Alice, Beefer, Stew, Bill, Mikey, Mikey's husband, Reb, Sue, the asshole—turning around and around in a lot of black space.

They Always Want to Eat Something

When I was a waitress a man and a woman came in every Thursday at noon. They sat at the same table and talked. They were having an affair. I considered it my job, at that period of my life, to serve people food and observe them. It was my job to observe life and love in Toronto, in the 1980s. Now I'm an editor. Hubba bubba.

The man and the woman were real-estate agents, realtors. Real-a-tors, they called themselves. It always sounded to me like mat-a-dors.

Some people have said I am not kind. Me, unkind, ungenerous, living with my teenage son in a cramped but funky Annex suite. The people who said that wanted sympathy when their marriages fell apart. They wanted sympathy and a warm bed, the men and women alike. But when I say, Oh, oh, oh, I'm sorry you didn't communicate your needs to one another (that is, had no fucking self-knowledge), I feel like I'm falling and the drop never ends. Apparently when you fall into a black hole time stops and you get stretched out like a piece of spaghetti until you're nothing, and the future is just a grand show of particles exploding in fountains of colour and light at the edge of the event horizon. When I say, Oh, oh, oh, I feel like I've gone down. I once went on a binge of Woody Allen movies, eating up his prying sexual wit, his charming neurotic characters fizzling out in beautiful clothes, in daring, minuscule acts of self-revelation and courage.

I've said that the matadors were having an affair, but there was no heat rising up between them to resist the swooping in of my hand bearing fragrant hummus and pita. It was for that I hated them most of all. They had new ways of arranging information on their computers and became flushed as they discussed moving x to y and conflating f with g. You could do so many things.

The man was blond, clean-cut, and wore perplexing layers of beige. I know they were layers, because I know the difference between a shirt and a vest and a jacket. But they *looked* like one mean smooth topography, a flat desert of good cloth. He had three children, and his wife had dark wavy hair and was fifteen pounds overweight. This wife had been wholesome looking when they got married, he said. He had mistaken a slight dip under her cheekbones for aristocratic force, but now realized that she had never been exotic or European in any way.

The woman was also blond, clean-cut, and wore layers of beige. To me, she did not look exotic or European in any way. She was not and had not ever been married. She ate carefully, small portions, and kept his attention with hers.

He talked about local doctors and lawyers entwined in scandals, fiscal and otherwise. He talked about his mortgage, what she should do about her mortgage, and occasionally even my mortgage, which I didn't have. She agreed that Dr. B. had not contributed enough to the building of the new library, and that the warnings about butter were exaggerated, though not much.

They didn't call food "food," but "calories." Things like, "I met with Bishop this morning, but I was shaky, too low on calories I think, and I didn't grind the deal." They also called protein "prote." It sounded like his tennis partners with their blunt, hacked-off names.

"Grab a life," my teenage son would say, but he would laugh when I described the man and the woman. He would sit there across the breakfast nook from me, wolfing down three or four sandwiches and a quart of milk at a time. It was gratifying to think of the food working its way into muscle and bone. He would wolf, and sit there grinning at me while I detailed what he said and what she said and what he said.

Just once, I went to a New Age therapist.

"Is it because they have money that you hate them?" she said, blue eyes wide with the effort of calm knowing. "That they dare to gather around them the abundance you do not?"

He too ate small portions, and occasionally patted his tidy stomach as the last mouthfuls went down. They both had coffee with steamed milk, not cream.

"I've had this idea," I told the therapist, "that materialists hate matter, really hate it." The therapist blinked one slow blink and, in the lilt of a bad kindergarten teacher, said that I was moving into the realm of abstractions, and away from my real issues—the starvation of my inner money-maker, my conduit to abundance.

Hairdressers in T.O. are expensive, so to save money I always went to a hairdressing school. The students would come and go, some cuts were good, other cuts were bad. Some students would hold the hair timidly between two fingers, not even stretching out the wave, and you knew it would be bad. But for a few months I had the most confident pair of hands in town weaving through my hair—honestly, you couldn't tell the haircutting from the haircut. This beautiful set of fingers belonged to a short, stocky lesbian with a Cheshire cat grin. She teetered on the edge of sanity, her conversation swooping up like a skateboarder on the domed edge of our brief time together. I saw the faint scars on her wrists as she bent over me.

This is how she did it: she would stand there behind the head in the mirror in combat pose with the scissors poised. She would scan her cut for imperfections, for tiny, subtle flaws in the lying flat or the standing up or the degree of fluffy or the dramatic angle. She would find the flaw and then point with the scissors, firmly declaring "That." She loved to seek and find, to go deeply into the troubled waters of form. About hair, she was never wrong. She was an artist of the hairdressing dance—snip, "That," snip, "That!"

At the restaurant, we'd always keep fresh flowers on the table. Every day, new kinds of flowers. One day, Thursday, it was white mums. The man and the woman called me to their table just after they had settled.

He said, "Please take these away. Mums sap my masculinity." For one glorious firecracker of a moment, I thought he was being funny. I looked at him, my open face ready to meet his mirth. But nobody was there, and he repeated, thinking I hadn't heard, "Please take these away. Mums sap my masculinity."

Then mums have a lot of company in this world, I thought, and lifted the snowy glassful.

It was one of their own conversations that finally freed me from them one day, because I no longer needed to think of them as anything at all. It went like this:

He: Oh yes, Linda's such a hard worker, in the office at seven every morning, sometimes before. She gives a hundred and fifty percent, always. A winner, that girl.

She: Linda amazes me. She's the top seller a month out of every year. AND she has three kids. That's the part that gets me. How . . . with kids?

He: Well, I have three kids, and I know what it's like.

She: I know you have three kids. It amazes me. I can't imagine it, having kids. My friends with kids, it seems they spend all their time feeding them. It seems that those kids come bursting in from, well wherever kids come bursting in from . . . and they always want to EAT something!

He: Yes, they certainly have big appetites, that's for sure.

She (shaking her head, a dawning bovine pendulum of discovery, this, at least, her own): That's what gets me. *That*! They always want to eat something.

Civilization

At about the middle of a party last summer, Phillip told me that he had worshipped Dr. English and that he worshipped him no longer. Phillip is sweet and earnest and bright. Two children and his wife Alison surround him with a warm and fruitful aura. In it, he blooms and occasionally twists, dreaming of cool people-less libraries. His life is about changing pants and conjugal caresses and stolen Plato. He was the brightest student in our philosophy seminar with Dr. English. His papers were always late.

When Phillip told me this about Dr. English, Elvis Costello's "Alison" was coming out of the stereo speakers into the back yard.

"Alison. . . . My aim is true, my aim is true." Phillip

laughed. He and his wife were expecting another child. He is one of the purest human beings I know.

Dr. English thought evil was boring. I thought that it wasn't, so we didn't have much to say to each other. He gave me an A in Metaphysics, and I went on to study Ethics. To Phillip, he gave a B+ because Phillip's ideas did not, finally, resolve themselves into coherence. He foundered on Being.

Dr. English paced the floor, lectured on Aristotle's Unmoved Mover. He was interested in final causes that didn't budge. He had some admiration for Hegel, in the end, when Being knows itself. But he didn't like to think about all that writhing history in between. The indignity of it. Generally, he found the German philosophers turgid and distasteful.

Dr. English had, once, a seminar at his house. His wife was warm, friendly, and child-like. We were all titillated that there was a wife, and to hear Dr. English referred to as "Laurie." Dr. English stroked his cat, a skittish Siamese, with his delicate small fingers. His furniture was beige, his paintings tasteful and receding.

"I wanted to puke on the carpets," said Anna later. Anna was a dusky suntanned woman in her forties who seemed always to smell of sex. "No, I'd like to *shit* on those carpets. And let the wife out, send her on her way to a hot dance emporium in Italy."

When we were at Dr. English's house, I had gone to the bathroom and on my way noticed something on the floor of the bedroom, the door slightly ajar. It was a pair of balled socks, possibly dirty. I had a thrill.

At the end of spring, Dr. English gave a public lecture on Greek science. Beautifully formed ideas flowed in a pageant across the hour, and the audience nearly thundered applause at its close. I looked over to see Phillip, his eyes shining and cheeks flushed. Dr. English was glowing with pleasure as he left the stage. He was still glowing later in the day when I saw him in the lineup at Thrifty's. He was buying a single jar of artichokes, small and elegant. My twelve-pack of toilet tissue stuck out of the paper bag, ungainly as the problem of evil.

"Nice lecture today," I said.

"Thanks ever so much," he replied, setting the artichokes on the counter.

"Are you having a trip this summer?" I asked.

"Indeed. I'm going to the Bodleian to do research."

"How lovely," I said, and made my escape, disturbing a display topped with large cutout jungle figures.

"How did it come about?" I asked Phillip, meaning the end of worship.

"He had me to his house. We were discussing my inability to distinguish ontology from political theory. We talked about my paper, the one you read for me in the fall. I had got Being wrong again. He stopped a little suddenly and said that I mustn't let my family come in the way of my study. That I would be nothing, not a scholar. That's all. That's it, really. He's so polite, you know. He didn't mean to offend me."

"What a shit," I said.

"No. Not a shit. He just doesn't know." Phillip's blue eyes were steady, unmoving marbles. I looked for narrowing, for flickering. There was none.

Once, I was looking for Dr. English because I had a late paper from Phillip to submit. Phillip was with his children. I asked the department secretary for Dr. English's office hours, which I knew were not posted on his door.

"Dr. English was just here, and now he isn't," Margaret told me. "His office door is open, though, so I'll sign the paper and you can leave it on his desk."

The door was only very slightly open. I knocked, but there was no answer. I pushed the door and stepped over to drop the paper on the desk, but there were several documents already spread out there, so I had to look for a spot to put it. Finally, I dropped it right in the middle, on top of some papers, where I thought he would see it.

There were no photographs on the desk or walls, and of course no childish petroglyphs. There was something decorative, though. It was a drawing of the Acropolis, very good, in pen and ink, in a silver frame on the ledge facing the desk. The artist had caught the sheen of the dead white pillars, the way the sun burned and burned away all impurity.

One day in class Dr. English broke through an academic sound barrier, the modern convention that says that professors explain the thoughts of others but do not develop their own in front of students. It had almost happened a few times before, but this time he was launched, had finally broken free of the atmosphere. His eyes were bright, hot, as he soared away from an explanation of Aquinas' natural law and swooped into the realm of something he called Pure Thought. He said that Thought referred only to itself. It was not, however, at all true to say that Thought was thinking about itself. Thought was the fundamental ontological category, and, in fact, could not think about itself, because self-consciousness was divided and stuttering, and Thought was pure and unmoved, unruffled, and of course there are no paradoxes at the bottom of Truth. . . .

I wasn't really following. Phillip's hand shot up.

"What is the relation of Pure Thought to human community?"

Dr. English was not thinking about human community, particularly, but he didn't miss a beat.

"Civilization, real civilization would be," he said, slowly and carefully, "the thinking together of one great, clear thought. One lucid, pure, thought."

"What would the thought be about?" asked Phillip. He hadn't put his hand down the whole time.

Dr. English stopped pacing. He polished his glasses with his handkerchief and then put them back on.

"I'm afraid you've missed the whole point," quietly said Dr. English.

It was later in the party, after I had talked with Phillip about Dr. English, that Dr. English himself arrived. A small wire of excitement circuited the crowd. Other professors were present, were always present, at these parties, but Dr. English had never come.

I could see, right away, that there was something wrong. Dr. English was pale and unsteady on his feet, wearing the remains of a smile that had crashed. Slowly, a crowd accumulated around him. Anna was on the inside. As the hour went on, there was much hard, bright laughter, and I heard the words "wife" and "leaving" ricochet around the circle. There was much feeding of beer and wine, glass after glass, to Dr. English, much noise, much.

A moment came, I had heard it coming. The noise

resolved itself into stillness. Anna moved even closer to Dr. English. Anna pressed one red rayon hip against the hip of Dr. English. Dr. English was goofy and baffled and bleary. Anna said it, and everyone thought it with her, one great clear thought:

"Laurie, what you need is a good, wet . . ."

Phillip jumped forward.

"Stop it! STOP it!" He was hysterical, almost weeping. "Stop making him!"

Anna jeered. "You wanted him to be *human*," she hissed, twining her arms around the flopping torso of Dr. English. "Now he's *human*, part of human community."

It was dark now, and we were seeing by the string of small lights bobbing around the canopy above. Crickets chirped, a cat shot from house to yard. Phillip was still and white.

"That's not it. That's *not it*," he growled out like pain. He had no more words, I knew.

Anna twisted and writhed. Dr. English drooped and shuffled. And Phillip stood there glaring, rooted by his legs to the ground, two pillars of civilization.

Janina Hornosty was born in Vancouver in 1962. She attended McMaster University and York University and received her Ph.D. from McMaster in 1994. She has worked as a college teacher, a Girl Friday for a recycling company, and at a variety of "temp" jobs, including bookstore clerk, cleaner, and waitress. She currently teaches English and Liberal Arts at Malaspina College in Nanaimo, BC.